HER FAVORITE DUKE

THE 1797 CLUB, BOOK 2

JESS MICHAELS

Her Favorite Duke

The 1797 Club Book 2

For more information, contact Jess Michaels
www.AuthorJessMichaels.com

A special thank you to Mackenzie Walton
for all the extra help and support with this book.
A good editor is worth her weight in gold. You are platinum.

And for Michael who is and always will be my favorite duke, my favorite
person and my best friend.

AUTHOR'S NOTE

There are a lot of conversations about the concept of Content Warnings in books and for other media. Having suffered from panic attacks that were triggered by trauma, I would NEVER wish that on my worst enemy. I want you to enjoy what you're reading, never be pulled away because you were surprised by triggering material. So, I will do my best to include Content Warnings in an author note in each book from now on. Also, look to my website for them, so that you don't accidentally buy a book that might give you pause.

Content Warning: parental neglect (described, not on page), parental death (described, not on page), alcoholism.

PROLOGUE

1803

Margaret Rylon stood in her chamber wearing full black, a symbol of mourning. And she should be mourning, for her father had been put in the ground just a few hours before.

And yet, as she looked at herself in the glass, she did not see sadness in her eyes. She didn't feel it either. As much as his death should grieve her, she felt *nothing* in her heart for the late Duke of Abernathe. Why should she? The man had not actually spoken directly to her in three years, despite their living under the same roof. To him she had been nothing, a failure at an attempt at a spare.

To her he had been a cruel bastard. In truth, she was happy he was dead. Her brother James was duke now. And she adored James with all her heart.

It had always been the two of them against the world, really. Against a father who despised them, against a mother who dove headlong into a bottle to escape the fact that her husband despised her, too. Right now Meg was certain the duchess was fully lost in a drunken stupor and would probably remain that way for weeks, using the death of a husband she did not love as an excuse to spiral into darkness.

Meg sighed as she looked away from her reflection and paced to the window. Down below she saw the servants walking two horses toward the stables and her heart leapt, pushing away her troubled thoughts in an instant. The mounts could only mean one thing: Simon and Graham were here.

It had been six years since she'd met James's best friends, on a holiday from school when he'd been allowed to bring them home for a short stay. Although James had a whole club's worth of friends, it was Graham and Simon he spent the most time with. They were his best friends and she liked both of them.

But it wasn't both of them she thought about as she grinned down at the servants leading the mounts away. No, only one of those two men truly made her heart flutter. That was Simon Greene.

She closed her eyes and conjured an image of him without even trying. He was unbearably handsome, with a gorgeously angled face, thick dark hair and bright, expressive pale blue eyes. He was always smiling. Even when he wasn't smiling, the ghost of that expression was there. Like he was constantly thinking of a private joke.

When he looked at her, her heart skipped a beat. And he often looked at her. Across rooms, across tables, when they were walking. She might only be sixteen, but she knew when a man liked her.

A good thing, since she had accepted that she was in love with *him* a year ago. But it wasn't for a lady to take the first step. Her mother hardly ever gave her advice, but she'd slurred that out at some point when she caught Meg staring at Simon one night. The duchess wasn't wrong. A gentleman was to begin the courtship. One day he would. They had time, after all. She wasn't even out in Society officially yet. He was but nineteen, himself. They had all the time in the world.

She smoothed her skirts and went to the door. She walked down the hall and the stairs, smiling as she encountered the butler, Grimble, in the hall.

"Good afternoon. Where are my brother and his friends?"

Grimble inclined his head and straightened his black mourning band slightly. "His Grace is in his office with the Duke of Northfield. The Marquess Whitehall is in the west parlor, Lady Margaret."

Margaret flinched as she realized Grimble was referring to her *brother* as His Grace. That would take some getting used to. Of course, one day Simon would be "Your Graced" as well. He would be the Duke of Crestwood.

And to her, he would always be Simon.

She smiled at the butler. "Thank you, Grimble. As hostess, I'll seek out the marquess until my brother's business with Northfield is complete."

Grimble didn't really seem to care, but executed a sharp nod as she left him. Her heart began to pound as she opened the west parlor door. Simon didn't hear her as she entered, but remained in his place by the fire. He had one boot up on the hearth, his arm resting on the mantel. For a moment she couldn't see what he was looking at so intently, but when he moved his head, she caught her breath.

Her miniature was on the mantel and he was looking at it. Giddiness filled her and she cleared her throat softly to catch his attention.

He turned toward her and his face lit up. "Meg!" he said.

"Hello, Simon," she said, rushing into the room. She held out her hands as she approached him and he took them both, squeezing them gently as he did so. His hands were ungloved, as were hers, and she jolted with the shock of awareness that always came when he touched her.

"I'm sorry I couldn't talk to you at your father's service," Simon said as he guided her to a seat before the fire. "And I'm so terribly sorry for your loss."

Meg bent her head. "You know how Abernathe was...Abernathe

the last, I suppose now. I know it is meant for me to be sad, but how can I, Simon, when he didn't care a whit for me?"

Simon reached out and touched her hand lightly. "Then I'm sorry for that, Meg."

She smiled at his kindness. "My father will be the topic of most of my conversations for the next few weeks. So let's you and I discuss something else, shall we?"

He nodded. "Choose the topic, my lady, and I will attempt to be clever about it."

She laughed at his teasing. "Why is my brother having a secret meeting with Graham? I thought the three of you were inseparable."

For a moment, a shadow crossed Simon's face, and he frowned. "To be honest, I don't know what they're discussing. The moment we arrived James asked Graham to talk to him in private and I was not invited."

She wrinkled her brow at his expression. "Odd."

"Not as odd as you'd think," he said softly.

She shook her head. "I'm certain it's nothing. Maybe they're discussing surprising you for your birthday. It's a few months off still, but you can never plan too far ahead."

He chuckled, the storm clouds gone from his face. "And how do you know my birthday, Meg?"

"I remember everything about you, Simon," she admitted after a moment's hesitation.

He was silent except for a sharply inhaled breath. Slowly he turned toward her and her throat closed. He looked very serious suddenly and very focused on her. He opened his mouth as if to speak and she leaned in, hands shaking.

But before he could say a word, Grimble cleared his throat at the door and said, "Lady Margaret, His Grace requires your presence in his office."

She was yanked from the spell Simon had cast on her in a moment. She exchanged a look with him and then got to her feet, with Simon right behind her. "Very well, I'll join them momentarily."

The butler left and she looked at Simon. "Come with me?"

"I wasn't invited," he reminded her.

She shrugged. "*I* invited you."

He motioned for her to lead the way, and she did so. They walked together silently toward James's office, but it wasn't their usual companionable silence. All she could think about was what Simon could have intended to say before they were interrupted in the parlor.

James's office door was closed as she reached it and she knocked lightly before opening it to allow them in. She caught her breath as she entered. This had been her father's office before, of course, and it still looked and felt of him. Cold. Masculine. Unwelcoming. It didn't fit James, that was certain. She couldn't wait to help him make it over, stripping everything from the past away and welcoming a new future for them both.

Her brother was standing at the huge picture window with Graham, and they turned together as Simon and Meg entered. James was grinning, but Graham looked more reserved. He inclined his head ever so slightly toward her.

"Come in, Meg," James said, motioning her forward. "And Simon, good, you are here too. Excellent."

"Yes," Meg said. "Good afternoon, Graham. It's so nice to see you."

"Lady Margaret," Graham said, formal as always despite their longtime acquaintance. Today his voice was tight and he shifted slightly. Almost as if he were uncomfortable.

"I asked you to come in, Meg, because I have some news for you," James said, reaching out to take her arm and draw her closer. "Very happy news, I hope you'll agree."

Meg smiled. "We all need some happy news today. What is it?"

James looked at her face. Her brother's expression was intent and earnest and her breath caught at it even before he spoke again. "I have arranged a marriage for you, Meg."

Her smile faded as she stared at him. "A-a marriage?" she repeated, certain she had misheard him.

He nodded swiftly and the excitement in his tone increased. "I realize I didn't speak to you about it before, but I have been thinking of nothing else for weeks, since Father took ill."

She tried to catch her breath as she looked back over her shoulder at Simon. He was standing stock still, staring at James, not looking at her. His expression was entirely unreadable.

"I wanted to know you would be taken care of, Meg," James continued. "In case I'm ever in a position where I could not do it."

"James—" she began.

"And it is with a friend," he pressed forward, ignoring her interruption. "Someone we both like. Someone I *know* will have only your best interest at heart."

Now her heart leapt. Could he possibly be talking about Simon? He had wanted to say something to her in the parlor. Could it have been a desire to share the news privately, and all his talk of not knowing the subject of James's discussion with Graham was a ruse?

"Who?" she asked, breathless as she hoped, prayed…

James guided her forward until she was standing before Graham and suddenly everything became clear. Her heart sank, her blood ran cold and it suddenly felt like time slowed.

"Graham and I have just finished the arrangements, Margaret. You are engaged to the Duke of Northfield."

Her lips parted as she stared at Graham. His blue eyes were locked on hers, but there was no joy in them. His lips were a thin line of resolution. He didn't seem unhappy, but there was no excitement or emotion in his stiff expression.

He reached out and suddenly her hand was in his. Unlike when Simon had taken it, there was no spark to the action. He cleared his throat and said, "I will endeavor to make you happy, Margaret."

He lifted her hand to his lips and they brushed softly across her skin. As he did so, she looked again at Simon. He was looking at the floor now, seeming entirely bored by this exchange. When he looked up and caught her eye, he smiled at her.

"Congratulations, Margaret," he said. "Graham."

He moved forward and the three men began shaking hands and slapping backs. She stared in mute shock as they did so. Here she had always thought the attraction she felt toward Simon was returned, but he made no effort to protest this engagement. In fact, he didn't look like the idea of it even meant anything to him in the slightest.

Could she have misread him so badly?

"Are you happy?" James asked as he leaned in to buss her cheek.

She looked up into her older brother's eyes. He had just had so much placed on his shoulders as the new duke. This was the first time since their father's illness that he'd looked happy in the slightest.

She glanced past him at Graham. No one could say he wasn't handsome. And they had been friendly in the past. If Simon didn't want her, she could do worse. And she'd have many years to grow accustomed to the engagement before they'd be wed.

She nodded and forced herself to smile. "Of course, James. I'm... I'm very happy."

He seemed to accept that answer and hugged her before he rushed to the sideboard to pour drinks of celebration for them all. She swallowed and looked out into the garden behind the house.

She would forget Simon and her silly notion that he cared for her. She would forget. It seemed she would have to.

CHAPTER 1

Seven Years Later

Simon Green, Duke of Crestwood, stood in the middle of the ballroom, staring at the couples dancing. Well, that wasn't *exactly* true. He was actually staring at just one couple dancing. Lady Margaret, sister to one of his closest friends, and her fiancé, Graham Everly, Duke of Northfield. It was a rare thing to see them together, for Graham always cried off the duty. He didn't like to dance.

Meg did. She was good at it, too. Simon knew because she often came to him to dance when her fiancé would not. It was so easy to slip his arms around her and guide her around the floor as she stared up into his eyes and talked to him about everything and nothing. He could almost feel her in his arms right now. Warm and soft and his.

He blinked and shook his head. This needed to stop. But then, he'd been telling himself that same thing for years, and it never did. If anything, it only got worse and worse.

"I'm surprised you aren't dancing, Crestwood."

Simon turned, a smile turning up his lips at the approach of the

Duke and Duchess of Abernathe and the Earl of Idlewood. James and Christopher, who many called Kit, were two of his dearest friends, and Emma was James's new bride. The men all belonged to the 1797 Club, a small collection of their closest friends who had all become dukes sometime in the past decade. Well, except for Kit. He had not yet ascended to the title, not that he or anyone else was sad about that fact. His father was the greatest and best of men.

"I did not find a suitable partner for the quadrille," he said.

Emma looked out at the crowd. "Yes, the room is bereft of partners, for sure," she teased gently as she motioned toward the room half full of beautiful women.

Simon turned toward her slightly and winked. "I don't suppose *you* would like to take a turn, Your Grace?"

Emma blushed and laughed at his playful flirtation, and James drew her a little closer with an equally teasing glare in Simon's direction. "Careful now. We are newlyweds and I am wildly jealous. *You* need to find your own partner."

Simon's smile faded a fraction and he looked once more at Meg. She was laughing now at something Graham had said, her brown eyes lit up, her head tipped back so loose tendrils of dark chestnut hair danced along her shoulders.

She looked happy.

Simon sighed. He knew James was right in his assessment of the situation. At some point, Simon just had to forget the feelings he had for his friend's fiancée and move on with his life.

"I shall endeavor to do as you say," Simon said.

"It seems that since James and Her Grace have taken the plunge, it will likely be all of us who follow," Kit said with a barely imperceptible sigh. "Our little group is of an age now."

"Meg and Graham will be next, I'm certain," James said, looking out at his sister and their friend with a beam of happiness.

Simon flinched away from it. It had been seven years since he stood in a room in this very house and listened to James declare that he had arranged for Margaret to marry Graham. How well Simon recalled that horrible moment when those words had come from his lips. How they had echoed in the room around them all. How his ears had begun to ring, making every word sound like it came from far away or under water.

How well he remembered Meg stepping toward Graham, away from him, and the way his chest had burned with anger and jealousy and loss. And then he'd looked at James's face. James, who was his brother in every way but blood.

And James had looked so damned happy. So certain that he was doing the right thing. So pleased to do something for Meg. For Graham.

Simon hadn't been able to destroy his friend's plans in that moment. And later, after the engagement was happily announced in every paper and ballroom in the country, he couldn't destroy those plans for fear of destroying Meg along with them.

So he'd kept his feelings to himself. Swallowed them down deep where they couldn't tear the world to shreds. And he'd waited for Meg and Graham to marry.

Only they hadn't. Yet. Still. And now he looked at James, who was whispering something in Emma's ear. He saw the love his friend felt for his new bride, and that jealousy and anger and pain burned bright again. He wanted what they had.

He wanted it with Margaret. Just as he had since he was nineteen.

"—a waltz," James was now saying, his words drawing Simon from his dangerous thoughts. "And my wife and I are going to dance it. You and Simon should find partners, too, Idlewood."

He smiled as he took Emma's hand and led her to the dance floor. Once they were gone, Simon let out a long breath. Not just because he had survived a very uncomfortable conversation but because Meg and Graham had left the dance floor and immediately parted. Meg had gone to talk to a few friends, Graham headed for the terrace. At least Simon would not have to see them move together in the infinitely more intimate waltz.

"You are staring at her," Kit said from beside him.

Simon jolted. "Who?"

Idelwood turned toward him, arms crossed. "Margaret."

Simon froze, staring up at his friend and trying to read whatever he knew. But Kit's face was impassive in that moment.

"Well, she has been my friend for a very long time, hasn't she?" he asked, reverting back to the same explanation he gave whenever someone asked him about Margaret. The words weren't untrue. Since her engagement to Graham, he and Meg had become closer. Friends.

He would venture to say, though never out loud, that she was his best friend.

Kit tilted his head slightly, his expression filled with dangerous disbelief. "I've known you a long time. I've known *her* a long time, too. And...it's more than that, isn't it?"

"I don't know what you mean," Simon said, setting his jaw as he made to walk away. Kit darted a hand out and caught his arm.

"I wouldn't say a damned thing," he said softly. "You are my friend and it's clear from the way you're standing there, shifting in your place and unable to look at anything but her, that you are struggling. So what is it? Tell me and I swear on all I hold dear that I will never breathe a word of it to anyone. *Anyone.*"

Simon shut his eyes briefly. What Christopher offered was a boon, indeed, for he had no one else to talk to about this. Not James or Graham, certainly. Nor the rest of their tight group of friends, either, for they had all pledged such loyalty to each other. He wasn't certain he wouldn't be shunned for admitting he coveted what Graham had.

He sighed. "You may not be wrong," he said carefully, watching Kit's face for a flash of judgment and horror. There was none. "But there is nothing that can be done about it, is there? Meg was long ago promised to a man I consider as close as blood, and by another I hold just as dear. To pursue or even admit what I feel...it would destroy everything and everyone I love. Including her."

Kit's expression softened. "How long have you felt this way?"

"Forever," he whispered. "Seven or eight years."

"But you...you were whoring around London with Roseford back then, almost coming to blows over women you bedded."

Simon flinched. "I had my fun, yes. I wasn't ready to settle down. And I...I missed my opportunity. Or maybe there never was one. Even if I had been a choirboy, perhaps James still would have chosen Graham to match to Margaret. Because they're closer friends."

He looked out at James and Emma, close together, eyes locked on each other as they twirled. They looked blissful. Simon loved and hated them for it.

"I'm sorry," Kit said and it was clearly genuine. "I can well imagine how painful it would be to watch the woman I loved marry someone else. Especially a friend."

Simon shrugged. It felt a little better to say something out loud about the subject. But it changed nothing.

"In the end, James is right," he sighed. "We must all begin to do our duty. To marry and produce the heirs that will take our place. So I suppose the best thing I can do is forget this foolishness with Meg and get about doing it."

"So you should dance," Kit said gently.

"Yes," Simon said, clapping a hand on his friend's shoulder. "I should dance."

But as he peered out over the crowd, looking for the lady he would do just that with, his heart sank. When he spoke of the future, he could never picture anyone but Meg by his side.

And that was the place she would never, never be.

Margaret hated Sarah Carlton. Oh, she had never hated her before. She hardly knew her well enough to feel one way or another about her. But now, as the other young woman was dancing in Simon's arms, leaning up into him to talk above the music, Meg hated her.

And hated herself even more for feeling so strongly about her. About Simon.

She turned to look at the man who stood by her side. Graham Everly, Duke of Northridge, was everything a lady could desire. Only she didn't, despite the fact that he was devilishly handsome, with blond hair that was just a little too long, bright blue eyes and a smile that lit up a room. Well, when he did smile, which he had done less and less frequently as of late.

Even now, as he caught her staring, he shifted with discomfort under her attention rather than seeming pleased with it.

"Do you need something?" he asked, ever solicitous. Her friends were so very jealous of that fact. "A drink? Some air?"

She sighed and looked out of the corner of her eye at Simon again. He was laughing and she wanted to slap his pretty dance partner right across the face. "Yes," she said. "Air, I think, would do me good."

He nodded, taking her arm and guiding her through the crowd and out onto the terrace. He released her immediately, and she walked to the terrace wall and drew a few long breaths to steady her nerves.

Then she faced her fiancé. He wasn't looking at her, but worrying a loose thread on the hem of his sleeve. She took the moment to really observe him. Once upon a time, she had liked Graham a great deal. She'd considered him a friend, and once she'd resigned herself to their engagement, she had hoped she would one day see him as more.

But it had been seven years and if anything, they had only drifted further and further apart. They did not talk beyond the surface of most subjects. They did not laugh. And he certainly never made any attempts to touch her or to kiss her.

When she lay in bed at night, it wasn't him who visited her in her dreams, either. That was Simon. Still and always and forever.

She hated herself for it, more than she hated any woman Simon had ever paid attention to for more than a few moments. She hated herself because she knew her feelings for Simon were wrong.

She cleared her throat and stepped closer to her fiancé. "James and Emma seem very happy," she said.

He lifted his gaze and his lips tilted ever-so-slightly in a soft smile. A true smile, and her heart softened a bit toward him. Graham had always loved her brother. *That* she appreciated more than anything.

"They do," he said, looking back over his shoulder to the ballroom, where James was dancing yet again with his wife. "Despite all the drama that led up to their union, I cannot imagine he ever could have found a better match than he has in her."

"You know I agree with that. I adore Emma, I'm so pleased to have her as a sister. And they are the first in our set to marry, and their true happiness is a good example for us all."

He looked at her briefly, then back toward the ballroom. "It does make one think," he mused.

She faced him. "Think about what?"

He pressed his lips together and his hand wavered at his side, like he was thinking of taking hers but then changed his mind. "James wants us to marry."

She nodded. "Yes. Hence, the arrangement."

He shifted, his expression suddenly one of frustration. "No, I mean, he has spoken to me about it a few times since he wed, himself. His being settled seems to have increased his drive to see *our* engagement come to its conclusion."

Meg caught her breath. She'd only been sixteen when she and Graham's contract was signed. No one had expected them to wed immediately. But the years had slipped by and somehow she'd let herself be lulled into the safety that the marriage would never actually come.

Now it seemed Graham was about to change that.

"We've been engaged a long time, Meg," he said.

She could hardly breathe, but somehow she managed to croak out, "Seven years."

He cleared his throat and forced himself to meet her eyes. "Christmas."

She blinked. "I beg your pardon?"

"What do you think about marrying at Christmas? On my estate, with our friends and family in attendance?"

Meg's lips parted. Most women in her position would be thrilled at the idea of finally wedding their duke. Most would be even happier that he wanted a date that was only a few months away.

But to her, his words felt like a noose. Inescapable. Inevitable.

"Yes," she choked past a closed throat as tears stung her eyes. "That would be lovely and it gives me enough time to plan. Plus, it will be before Emma's baby comes, so she and James should still be able to travel."

Graham stared at her a long time, almost like he was seeing her for the first time. Then he bent his head and any attempt to make a connection with her was gone. "All right. I'll go in and speak to James about it. Will you join me?"

She shook her head. "No, I-I'd like to be in the cooler air a bit longer. I'll return shortly."

"Very good," he said, then turned away from her and walked into the ballroom, leaving her alone on the terrace.

She slipped away from the main area, around the corner of the house to a darkened corner outside an unused parlor. There a small table and chairs were set. She sank down into the seat and rested her arms on the table. Then she put her head down and began to weep.

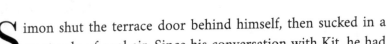

Simon shut the terrace door behind himself, then sucked in a great gulp of cool air. Since his conversation with Kit, he had felt this weight pressing down on him, crushing him. He hardly recalled the last twenty minutes. Hardly recalled the dances or his partners.

He didn't recall anything except for the pounding refrain that echoed in his head. *Margaret. Margaret. Margaret.*

He deserved to be called out for his obsession. He deserved to be abandoned. And yet he couldn't stop himself from thinking about her.

"I should leave," he murmured. "Go away for a few months or a few years."

He'd often thought that same thing, but he never followed through. Maybe it was time to finally do what was right. He bent his head and stared at his fingers, clenched against the stone wall of the terrace. He'd have to make a good excuse to go. He certainly couldn't tell Graham and James that he was desperately in love with Margaret.

He was still pondering that notion when he heard a faint sound echo from another part of the terrace. He turned, looking around as he did so. He was alone out here, or at least he'd thought he was. But now that he was attending, he heard more sounds. Sounds of…weeping.

He moved forward, toward the dark part of the terrace that was away from the windows and doors, around the corner and away from where anyone would easily find a person.

"Hello?" he called out as he stepped into the darkness and stopped, allowing his eyes to adjust now that light no longer filtered from the house. When they did, he gasped.

A woman sat at a table in the shadow of the house, her head resting down on her arms, and she was crying.

He rushed toward her. "I say, are you all right?"

For the first time, the unknown lady seemed to recognize his presence. She jerked her head up, turned her face toward him, and he screeched to a halt.

"Meg?" he whispered.

She didn't rise, but just stared up at him, her eyes unreadable in the half-dark. "Of course it would be you," she said, her voice thick with tears before she set her head back down.

He should have walked away. He should have gone inside and found her brother or her fiancé and let one of them comfort her as was appropriate.

But Meg had always been his friend as well as his obsession. And he wasn't about to walk away in her time of need.

He took a seat at the table, sliding it closer so that their legs brushed beneath the tabletop. Slowly, gently, he slid an arm around her shoulders and guided her toward him until she rested her cheek against his chest.

She let out a shuddering sigh, and the feel of her moving against him shot through him, waking every nerve ending, forcing him to face how desperately he wanted and adored her.

"What is it?" he asked, shocked he could form words when he was so damned aware of her in his arms.

She lifted a trembling hand and rested it against his heart. She could probably feel it pounding, even beneath all the layers of his clothing. He certainly felt the pressure of each and every one of her slender fingers.

"It's nothing," she said, her tone a little calmer now. "I was just overwhelmed for a moment."

He looked down at her and caught a whiff of the honeysuckle fragrance of her hair. God, how he loved that smell. He'd planted fourteen honeysuckle bushes around his estate in Crestwood five years ago just to have a tiny piece of her there with him.

"Did someone say something untoward to you?" he asked. "Because I'll go in there and—"

She tilted her face up toward his and his heart stopped. Her lips were three inches from his. Close enough that he could feel the faint stir of her breath against his mouth. Close enough that kissing her would be easy.

He *wanted* to kiss her. He wanted to do more than kiss her.

She swallowed, her eyes going a little wild as she gently

extracted herself from his arms, stood and walked out of the dark and into the safety of the light from the house.

"No one said anything," she whispered, her voice barely carrying.

He should have thanked her for moving them back into safety. What he wanted to do instead was catch her by the velvet sash around her waist and draw her back into the corner.

He got up and followed her. "You and I have been...*friends*...for a long time," he choked out. "You *know* you can tell me anything."

She stared up at him, and then her hand moved. He watched it as she lifted it and pressed in against his chest once more. Her fingers slid up and she brushed just the tips along his jaw. There was no breath between them, no space, and in that moment, there were no lies.

He could see something he'd spent years convincing himself didn't exist. Meg wanted him.

She pulled her hand away with a soft sound in the back of her throat and whispered, "I can't tell you *everything*, Simon."

"Meg," he ground out, moving to take her hand.

Before he could, the door opened behind them. Meg spun away, turning her back to him, her slender shoulders lifting and falling on panting breaths.

"Ah, there you two are."

Simon turned to smile as her brother stepped out onto the terrace with them. "James."

"We've been looking for you. Come inside, will you? We've an announcement."

Meg turned around and Simon caught his breath. She had composed herself to the point that no one would ever guess she had been weeping in the corner not five minutes before. She smiled brightly at her brother.

"Of course, James." As she passed Simon, she shot him a brief look. "Thank you for the—for the talk, Crestwood."

He nodded as he followed brother and sister into the house. "Of course, my lady."

James took her arm, leading her toward the small dais where the orchestra was playing. When he said something, they stopped, causing the dancers to halt and turn toward the cause of their interruption.

James shifted Meg so that she was standing beside Graham on the dais, and took Emma's hand, helping her into a place beside his own. Simon pushed through the crowd, coming closer as he tried to figure out what James could have to say. It was clearly a family announcement. Perhaps of Emma's pregnancy? James had already told his friends the happy news, but was this the proper forum to make it clear to the world?

But Emma looked just as uncertain as Simon felt as she slid a hand into the crook of James's elbow and awaited what he would say.

"Our family has been blessed with much good news as of late," James said. "And tonight I've a little more that I cannot wait to share. The Duke of Northridge and my sister, Lady Margaret—"

Simon jerked his face toward Meg. She was smiling, but her cheeks were pale, her eyes staring straight ahead.

"—will marry at Christmas!" James finished.

The crowd erupted in applause and talk, but Simon felt separated from all of it. He stood there, staring at Meg. She nodded as friends called out felicitations. She smiled into the crowd and once up at Graham.

But Simon knew her. He knew her and he'd seen her tears outside. *This* was why she'd been crying. This supposedly happy announcement of her impending wedding. After all this time, Meg didn't want to marry Graham.

And even though that should not have changed a thing for Simon, even though it should have only made him sorry for them both, instead it put a light of hope in his chest. It made him wonder if the future was cast in stone after all.

CHAPTER 2

M eg let her fingers move over the keys of her pianoforte, pouring out her emotion into the music in a way she could not pour out her emotions in real life. She put her anger there, her desperation, her heartbreak as she played, losing herself in the keys, forgetting the pounding fact that her wedding date was now set and marrying Graham suddenly felt very real.

She smashed her fingers down all at once and let out a strangled groan.

"Meg?"

She started as she turned to watch Emma slip into the music room, shutting the door behind her. Meg's cheeks burned as she looked away from her sister-in-law. "I missed a few notes."

Emma stared at her, silent for what felt like forever, then she moved to sit in one of the chairs beside the fire. She motioned for Meg to join her, and with a sigh Meg did so.

"You always play beautifully," Emma reassured her. "With more passion than most ladies I've watched play."

Meg held back a bark of frustrated laughter. "When she is sober, my mother calls my playing unseemly. Unladylike."

Emma's mouth pinched slightly at the mention of the dowager.

She was well aware of the issues the dowager had with drink. Not that very long ago, she had even helped Meg when her mother made a public scene. That had been the beginning of their friendship and eventually her relationship with James. The only thing Meg could thank her mother for.

"I think that having passion and being ladylike are not mutually exclusive," Emma said. "What is life without a little passion?"

She blushed as she said the words, and Meg smiled. "You would not have said that three months ago."

Emma laughed. "Perhaps not. Perhaps love gives us a different view on passion. I don't know."

Meg felt her smile slip away at the mention of love. She was truly happy Emma and James had found it, for her brother deserved nothing less than the devotion he'd found in the woman across from her. But seeing them so blissful only put her own situation in starker focus.

"What is troubling you?" Emma asked softly, her hand coming out to cover Meg's.

Meg sucked in her breath as pain mobbed her. Pain she pushed away with greater and greater difficulty. "Troubling me? Nothing, of course."

"I don't believe that's true." Emma's voice was very gentle. "You have not seemed happy since two nights ago, when the date for your marriage was announced."

"Why would I not be happy?" Meg choked out. "I will at last be Duchess of Northridge, just as my brother always desired."

Emma's brow wrinkled. "*James's* wish, yes. You always put it that way. But what about *your* wishes, Margaret? What are they?"

Meg pushed to her feet and walked away, for she had a great desire to simply scream out all that was in her heart. Right now the pressure of it was so great that she longed to spill it free where it could no longer torment her.

But when she looked at Emma, she saw more than a confidante and friend. More than a sympathetic ear.

"You are my brother's wife," she whispered. "Whatever I tell you will either go back to him or...or you'll be forced to keep it from him. I don't want to cause strife between you. I would never hurt my brother."

Emma's lips parted and she slowly rose, her hands outstretched. "This is very serious, isn't it? I can see it in your eyes, feel it in the way you tremble. Meg, your brother adores you. Let us go and talk to him about whatever it is that's troubling you. I'm certain we can work it out. That it can be fixed."

Before Meg could answer, the door behind them opened and the dowager entered the room. She jolted at finding the two of them standing so closely together.

"Was I interrupting?" her mother asked, and Meg was pleased that she did not sound drunk this afternoon. That was one less weight on her shoulders.

"No, we were finished," Meg said. "We were just talking about my playing."

Her mother glanced at the pianoforte. "Ah yes, I have not heard you play in an age, Meg."

Meg flinched, for she had played for the group not three nights before. That her mother did not recall that performance put her limitations in stark focus.

She smiled at Emma before she returned to the instrument. "Let me play for you now, Mother."

She took her place, set her fingers on the keys and began to play her mother's favorite song. Emma let out a soft sigh before she walked over to join the dowager beside Meg. As Meg played, she could feel her friend's stare burning into her back.

For once in the longest time, her mother had actually saved her from herself. From whatever would be caused if she lost her head and admitted her heart. Now as she played, she remembered herself.

Because she had to.

∽

Many nights, for many suppers, Simon had been placed beside or across from Meg. He had played the role of her good friend for so long that everyone expected them to chat and smile and rib each other good-naturedly. Even in gatherings outside their inner circle they were sometimes placed together. It came so very naturally.

Except for tonight. Tonight was different. Meg sat beside him, but she was not engaging in conversation with him. She wasn't smiling or laughing or teasing with him. She was staring at her plate, at her uneaten food, and seemed to be doing her level best to just get through this supper so she could leave his side.

That truth stung, especially after their intense encounter on the terrace two nights before. He'd thought it meant something. Now he wasn't certain.

"You are avoiding me, Lady Margaret."

She glanced up and met his stare, but her dark eyes darted away just as swiftly. "How can I avoid you when you loom up everywhere I go? Even now your elbow is in my space," she said.

He would have smiled at her statement, for this was a conversation they often had. Of course normally her words were said playfully. It was a game. Tonight her voice was dull and her body language closed and turned away from him so it brought him no pleasure.

He moved the offending elbow slowly. "Are you looking forward to the games tonight?" he asked.

She jerked her face back toward him, her eyes lighting up with something akin to...anger. Meg was angry with him? Why? He had done nothing to her that he could recall.

"Shall we retire to the parlor for cards?" Emma said, rising with a smile for James. "The gentlemen will take their port after."

The crowd rose, pairing off as one did at these things. Simon glanced down to see Graham taking the Dowager Duchess of Abernathe's arm, which left him free to escort Meg. He stood as she did, holding out his elbow.

"Walk with me?" he asked.

Once again there was a flicker of dark emotion across her face and she shrugged. "I suppose."

She didn't take his arm, though, as she had a dozen times, a hundred times. Instead she stepped out, trailing behind the others and leaving him to hustle to catch up with her. When he fell into step, he looked at her from the corner of his eye.

"Have I done something to offend you?" he asked.

She barked out a humorless laugh. "Never. Never once, Simon."

He wrinkled his brow at her sharp tone. He didn't understand it. He didn't want it. "Meg," he said, catching her arm and turning her toward him. "What is it?"

She blinked up at him, and once again there were tears sparkling in the corners of her eyes. She shook her head. "You are so blissfully unaware, Simon. I *wish* I could be like you."

"What does that mean?" he asked, his tone sharpening as his defenses came up. Her voice was so strained, her expression so hard and accusatory, but she would not explain herself, only make veiled accusations.

She carefully pulled her arm from his grasp and took a long step back. "It means nothing, Simon," she said with a sigh. "You have done nothing wrong. I am out of sorts. I apologize. Now I must catch up with the others. Just...just good night."

He watched her as she turned away and hurried up the hallway. He bent his head, uncertain if he should follow and continue this conversation or let her go. It was obvious she wanted nothing to do with him at present.

"Going to stand there all day or do you want to sneak into the parlor and have a bit of a drink with me?"

He turned to find Robert Smithton, Duke of Roseford, grinning at him. Once more Simon looked down the hall where Meg had gone, then he shrugged.

"It might be more fun than watching the games," he said.

"*Might?* You underestimate me, Crestwood," Robert said as he slung an arm around Simon's shoulder and all but dragged him to one of the adjoining rooms.

Simon shut the door as Roseford went to the sideboard and bent to shift the bottles beneath around. When he found what he sought, he let out a triumphant cry and lifted the bottle.

"Abernathe's best scotch," he said. "The one he hides away for special occasions." With a wicked grin, Robert poured them both a large portion and then set the bottle aside.

"And what special occasion are we toasting?" Simon asked, trying to drag his thoughts from his encounter with Meg and failing.

"The fact that when Abernathe comes in here and sees the bottle nearly empty, he'll curse our names?" Roseford teased. Then he lifted his glass with a shrug. "Or we could toast Northfield's upcoming marriage to Margaret, if you prefer to be more traditional."

Simon didn't lift his glass but took a long slug of the scotch wordlessly. Roseford arched a brow as he did so and then took his own sip. "You're pouting, Crestwood."

Simon swallowed and glared at his friend. "Pouting? I'm a grown man, we do not *pout*."

"Ask any governess. I'm certain she would recognize the signs right away," Roseford said.

Simon shook his head. "If you were alone with a governess, you wouldn't be asking her about me."

Robert laughed. "Not if she were comely, no. And damn it, man, you used to be right there with me! I could always depend on you to be at my side when conquest was on my mind. Hell, you remember that pretty opera singer in London?"

Simon clenched his jaw, for he did remember. Years ago, he and Robert had prowled for women together. They'd always found plenty of willing partners. They'd even shared a few of them, including the singer he now referred to. He supposed Robert meant for the memory to excite him.

It didn't. He thought of those times and knew what they really were to him. A way to forget Meg. A way that had never, *ever* worked, for here he was, just as in love with her as ever. Just as hopeless in that love as ever. The future just as determined as ever.

Roseford tilted his head and speared Simon with a closer look. Now his expression went from teasing to concerned. Simon's stomach turned. He'd already had a conversation about his heart with Idlewood—the last thing he wanted were words of comfort from Roseford of all people.

"You need to stop feeling this way," Roseford said, his jaw set and his tone sharp.

Simon wrinkled his brow. "What way?"

Roseford leaned back, incredulous. "Look, it is what it is. There is no changing it. So just *stop* feeling this way."

Simon's lips parted. "Just how many of you idiots think you know something about me and my heart?"

Roseford shrugged. "I don't know. It's a delicate subject, isn't it, you coveting what you cannot have. I'm certain some have noticed and others clearly have not or you would have been called out years ago."

Simon bent his head. "I deserve to be called out."

"Not unless you've done something," Robert said, slugging back another gulp of his drink. "Which I know you have too much honor to do."

"You say to stop feeling like the heart has a lever one can turn on and off," Simon said, pacing away. "It doesn't."

Roseford was quiet a long while, and then he shrugged. "I wouldn't know. I've never been so foolish as to let my heart lead. My cock, yes. My heart...no."

"So if I can't take your advice about shutting off how I feel, then what do you suggest I do?"

Roseford pondered the question for a moment, then his eyes lit up. "I know—let's go away."

"Go away?" Simon repeated. "Go away where?"

"Ireland, perhaps. The lasses there are always welcoming," Robert suggested. "Or...Napoleon's been quiet since his marriage. We might be able to sneak down to Italy, lie in the sun. You need a fuck and I'm certain we could manage that."

Simon chuckled even though he didn't truly feel in good humor. "Fuck the pain away, huh? Because it's worked so well before?"

"Maybe not, but it's worth a try, isn't it?" Roseford said. "Come on. It's been an age since we went on the prowl together."

Two days ago, Simon knew he would have refused this offer. The encounter with Meg on the terrace had given him a strange hope. But since she had been avoiding him ever since, and after that odd argument they'd had in the hallway, now he wasn't so sure.

She didn't seem to want him to intrude upon her arrangement, even if he could see she wasn't happy with it. And the consequences for doing so would be so grave. Graham would despise him, likely James too. And certainly none of the others would appreciate that he would go against one of their group.

Loyalty was important. His was being tested. But if Meg didn't want him...

"Very well," he said softly.

Roseford's eyes went wide. "Really?"

"Yes, perhaps you're right that I need a change of scenery." He allowed himself a heavy sigh. "I do have one request, though."

"And what is that?" Robert asked.

"I want to leave soon," Simon said. "I want to leave soon, and I don't want to come back until after Northridge's wedding."

Roseford wasn't exactly the most empathetic of their group, but his face softened at the request. He nodded slowly. "Of course, Crestwood. If that is what you need, I'll begin making arrangements right away. We could leave in a few days' time and certainly we can find plenty to do that wouldn't bring us home until long after the new year."

Simon wanted to feel relief in this decision. After all, he was about to keep himself from doing something he might regret. And yet, as he clinked his glass against Robert's, he didn't feel good.

He felt like he was running away from his future. He felt like he was running away from his heart.

CHAPTER 3

Simon couldn't help his smile as he watched Meg wallop the croquet ball with all her might. She had always been competitive and her laughter carried through the air, caressing his ear like a kiss. He *would* miss this when he was gone. Just as he would miss the soft music of her voice, the way tendrils of hair shivered around her face when she moved, the way she always let her hand linger on his a beat too long when they met or talked or danced.

He shook his head, trying to shake off these feelings. Needing to do so now more than ever.

The thoughts, though, were persistent and they grew even more intense as he caught sight of Graham moving through the crowd, his gaze focused on Simon. Simon tensed as Graham reached him and took a place beside him to watch the game on the lawn continue.

"Crestwood," Graham said softly.

Simon flinched. They used to all call each other by their first names, he and James and Graham. Somewhere along the way in the last few years, Graham had become more formal with him. Perhaps he sensed what Simon tried to hide, but he'd never said a word about it.

They hardly said a word to each other at all anymore, unless James orchestrated it.

"Graham," Simon said. "Enjoying the party?"

Graham hesitated a moment, just a flash of time but long enough that Simon sent a side glance at him. Graham was watching Meg, but he wasn't smiling.

"It is a party, much like many others."

"I suppose," Simon agreed. "And yet this one is different, at least for you."

"How so?" Graham asked, facing him with question in his eyes.

Simon swallowed, shocked that Graham didn't realize the most important thing in his life had happened here. "You and Meg. You've chosen your date to marry."

"Ah." Graham shook his head. "Of course. Yes. I suppose that does make the party special."

Simon clenched his fists at his sides and slowly tried to calm his racing heart. He could not understand Graham. He'd been engaged to Meg for years, yet he didn't seem to make any effort to connect with her. If he had been any other man in the world, Simon would have challenged him for her. He would have stolen her if he had to.

But Graham wasn't just any other man. He was one of Simon's closest friends.

Simon watched as Meg straightened and stepped back to allow the next lady to take her shot. Her gaze slipped across the lawn and when she found Simon and Graham, the smile that had brightened her face fell. Her cheeks paled. And Simon saw, yet again, that same desperate expression she'd had on the terrace a few nights before.

His heart clenched at it.

"Is Meg...is Meg all right?" he asked softly.

The question seemed to startle Graham and he turned his attention to his fiancée. He shrugged. "She looks fine to me. Why? Did she turn an ankle?"

"No," Simon said. "I mean, is she well? Is she...happy?"

"Of course," Graham answered swiftly, without even considering the question. "Why would you ask such a thing?"

Simon knew he should leave it at that. That he should say it was nothing and back away before Graham saw what Kit and Roseford already claimed to know. And yet, as he glanced once more at Meg, saw the tug of a frown on her mouth, he found he couldn't.

He drew a long breath. "Just...her spark seems dull, don't you think?"

Graham didn't look at Meg again. Instead he kept his stare firmly on Simon's face. Simon stiffened at the intensity of his friend's glare and found his body clenching, as if readying for a fight.

The silence stretched between them for what felt like forever, and then Graham said, "She seems *fine* to me."

Graham's voice was soft, but dangerously so, and firm. In that moment Simon realized he was in a battle. And if he didn't behave carefully, his house of cards would be destroyed around him.

He moved closer and saw Graham stiffen just as he had a moment ago. His chest ached with how far apart they had grown. Because of him. This was *his* fault.

"Graham, your friendship means a great deal to me," he said in a rush of words.

Graham nodded slowly, cautiously. "As yours does to me. I would not want anything to come between us. And I know Margaret values your friendship, as well."

Simon fought the urge to step back from that statement. That reminder that he could not, would not, ever be more to Meg than what he was today.

He clenched his teeth as he looked at her. She had set her mallet aside now and stepped away from the game. "Yes, we have always been...*friends*," he conceded slowly.

Graham tilted his head, forcing Simon to look at him. His expression held no anger, but it was hard. Cool. "You cannot interfere with what James has planned, Simon. It *is* what will happen. It is far too late to change it now."

Heat rose up in Simon, flushing his face and pumping blood through his veins all the faster. He knew this feeling and he hated it. It was rage. Rage directed toward Graham for what he said. Rage that Graham had what Simon had always wanted, rage that Graham didn't seem to appreciate the gift he had been given all those years ago. And rage that Graham would question Simon's loyalty. Simon, who had stood by mute as the woman he loved was taken from him by a friend he considered a brother.

He wanted to lash out at Graham. Verbally, physically. He wanted to strike at him, and he hated himself for it.

"I have *never* interfered," he growled instead.

Graham arched a brow and was quiet a moment before he said, "Of course." He turned away from Simon, and the tension of the encounter faded slightly when they were no longer face to face. "Excuse me. I think I see James motioning for me. Good afternoon, Crestwood."

He walked away then, without a look back. Without another word. And Simon stared at him as he did it, wishing he could call his friend back and repair this rift between them. Knowing he couldn't until he overcame his feelings for Meg.

The game on the lawn was over now and he sought her out in the crowd. She had not swarmed forward with the rest to congratulate the winner. She stood off to the side, her head bent and her hands clenched at her sides. She looked so very troubled, so very unhappy. But no one else seemed to notice. No friend or family member or fiancé rushed to comfort her. She stood alone and still until she lifted her head and let her gaze shift, slowly but purposefully, to him.

They were far apart. He on the stone courtyard just outside the yard perimeter, she on the other side of the playing field, and yet the connection that had always drawn him to her was strong as ever. It was like she had him on a string and all she had to do was look at him to make him move toward her.

Today he took a step in her direction and she ducked her head, breaking the gaze before he could take another. She shook her head slowly and walked away. She walked away from the players, away from the garden, away from the house and away from him.

And there was no doubt as to what he would do next. He would follow. Even though he knew it was interfering to do so, even though he knew it was stupid and foolish. Worse, it was wrong. It wasn't his place. And it could lead to something he would not be able to take back.

But he was going to follow her despite all that. Because soon he would be gone and there would be no further opportunity to do so.

As for the consequences of such an action, for the moment he chose not to think of them. Or if he did, he chose not to care.

M eg had been walking for an hour. She had no destination in her mind, she had no plan, she just walked, enjoying the sun on her face when it peeked from behind the gray clouds and the breeze that stirred her hair and skin when it spun up around her.

She was free. In these moments, she was free. And yet she felt the prison walls that would soon be her life closing down around her.

She stopped in the middle of the woods where she had wandered and leaned one hand against a tree as she struggled to regain the composure that was threatening to fray like a shawl that had been pulled and tugged too long and too hard.

Simon and Graham had stood together, talking as she played croquet. She'd seen them looking at her, seen Simon's gentleness and Graham's faint disinterest. All the emotion she constantly fought to keep down had risen in her in that moment, and suddenly nothing had mattered except escaping them both.

Escaping everything.

"But you can't escape," she said out loud, her tone harsh as she clenched her fingers against the rough bark of the tree. "This is what your life is and there is…no…changing…it."

The last three words were broken as she whispered them because her breath suddenly became short and her chest tightened with the thought. She bent her head and fought the tears that threatened to fall. She had wept enough these past few days. This was enough. She had to accept the future and stop being a ninny about it.

There was nothing in heaven or on earth that would change what was about to happen.

"Meg."

She stiffened at the sound of her name behind her, spoken in a voice she knew as well as any in the world. The only voice that had ever mattered.

Simon, she mouthed without daring to say his name out loud. If she did, then this fantasy that he was here with her would be shattered.

Slowly she turned, and her heart skipped in a way it should not. Simon *was* there. He wasn't any fantasy or illusion created by her errant mind. He was there, standing ten feet away, watching her.

"Are you following me?" she gasped out, her tone sharper than she had intended in her shock.

His full lips turned down into a deep frown. "Yes," he snapped back, also sharp. He had never spoken to her like that before, and it made her jump. "For an hour."

"Why?" she asked.

He arched a brow. "Because I—"

He cut himself off abruptly and turned his face from hers. She folded her arms and waited for him to continue. Waited for him to speak. To say *anything*.

"I saw you leave the gathering," he finally whispered, his shoulders rolling forward as if he were defeated. "And I thought you shouldn't be alone."

She took a step toward him. "Wh-why?" she stammered.

He lifted his gaze back to her. Their eyes met, and suddenly he straightened and his gaze grew heated. How many times had she seen that warmth in his eyes, that connection, when he looked at her? Every other time he'd pushed it away and she had told herself over and over again that it was only something she imagined even though she knew in her heart it wasn't true.

Today when they were alone, far from the others, far from whatever propriety dictated, that heat stayed and her body reacted just as it shouldn't. She tingled from her head to her toes, but especially in forbidden places. Places she touched while she thought of this man.

She shivered and forced those thoughts away.

"Why did you follow me?" she repeated.

"Because of a few nights ago," he said. "When you were crying on the terrace. I-I know you aren't happy, Meg. I know you—"

She barked out what she knew was an unladylike burst of laughter. "What do you know?" she asked, taking another long step toward him. The distance between them wasn't quite closed but it was narrowed significantly now.

His eyes widened as she did so, and it was clear he was aware of the challenge she was putting forward to him. She didn't care anymore, at least not in that moment. She was playing with fire, and getting burned was the least of her worries. She wanted him to do something.

Anything.

And it seemed like he might. In this magical stolen moment in the woods, he raised a trembling hand, his fingers reaching for her. She held her breath as she waited, her body strung tight and ready for whatever would come next.

Thunder rolled around them and the spell was broken. Simon jerked his hand away and lifted his gaze to the increasingly gray sky. "It's going to rain, Meg," he said. "We should go back."

She pursed her lips, glaring at the offending sky that had kept her from having what she wanted. Or perhaps saved her from doing something foolish. She supposed it could be seen from either perspective.

"Once we go back, it is over," she said, to herself, but also to him. "It's *over*. The future is irrevocably set."

He held her stare and emotions she had never seen from him washed over his face. Regret was chief amongst them, and a vise tightened around her heart at the sight of it.

"Meg," he whispered. "It has always been irrevocably set."

Her shoulders rolled forward and she let out a shuddering sigh. "Yes, you're right. Of course you're right. Then let us go. As you said, the rain is coming. We shouldn't get caught out in it."

Simon walked beside Meg, just as he'd done so many times before. Only today there was a tension between them, a push-and-pull they had never allowed into the light until a few days before. Now it sat there, a barrier to their friendship and a window into his soul that he knew was so very dangerous to uncover.

Worse, it was a window into *her* soul. For the second time in as many days, he saw clearly that she wanted him too. It had been lit up in her eyes and drawn across her face. Margaret Rylon wanted him.

And he couldn't do a damned thing about it, because she was Graham's.

"He'll take care of you," he said, the words sounding hollow in the quiet of the woods. "Graham will take care of you for all your days."

She spun on him, her eyes sparking with anger and other emotions that he saw and couldn't quite believe. "Is that supposed to comfort me?" she snapped. "That he will take care of me? Like I am an animal to be fed and watered and that is enough?"

"That isn't what I meant," Simon said.

She waved him off. "I have *never* believed that Graham would make a poor husband. He is a good man, a decent man, a strong man. A very handsome man."

Simon flinched at her recitation of his best friend's better qualities.

"But I *don't want him*," she finished. "James chose him for me all those years ago and I know he had his reasons for doing so. But I *never* wanted him." She caught her breath on a sob and took a step toward Simon. "I wanted...I only wanted..."

"Don't say it," he whispered, knowing that if those words left her lips he would lose all ability to control himself. He would lose any loyalty he felt to his friends and he would touch her. Once he started, he feared he'd never stop.

He should have left a week ago. He should have never come here at all. Certainly he shouldn't have followed her because there had been some part of him that had known this would happen.

But here he was and she was staring up at him with wide, wanting eyes.

In that moment, the rain began. Not in a trickle, but a torrent that cascaded from the sky. She yelped out a sound of surprise as the cool water hit her.

Simon hunched against the downpour and grabbed Meg's hand. "Run!" he cried.

He felt her fingers tighten in his own as they bolted down the path toward the house miles away. She began to laugh and he couldn't help but join her.

And for one brief moment, it was heaven.

CHAPTER 4

M eg was in hell. A cold, wet hell. The walk that had taken an hour going out was clearly going to take twice that getting back thanks to the pouring rain, blowing wind and muddy paths. She and Simon had been slogging through it for twenty minutes and she was soaked all the way through to her skin.

Her very cold and miserable skin. And God, but her gown was heavy. It felt like it weighed fifty pounds as it molded to her body.

The only positive thing in all this was that Simon still held her hand as he guided her on the way back home. She clung to his strong fingers, and in the moments when they slid against her cold skin, she wished their walk would never end.

Even if they were both going to catch their death from it.

"Bollocks," he muttered, his words barely carrying back to her over the roar of the wind and the pounding of the rain.

"What is it?" she asked.

He pivoted toward her. The rain had flattened his hair against his forehead and rivulets glided down his angular cheeks. She caught her breath. Wet Simon was also an utterly beautiful Simon.

If he noticed something different in her stare, he didn't react to it. In fact, he pressed his lips together in displeasure and said, "The little stream you crossed over on your way out?"

"Yes?" she said. There was a small bridge over it, built by her grandfather decades ago, before she was born.

"Well…" Simon trailed off and motioned his hand forward.

She stepped up, squinting through the torrent, and caught her breath. The stream was now a raging river, water pouring over the bridge and cutting off their path.

"Oh God," she groaned. "We're going to have to go all the way around to Glassford Hill to circumvent the stream! It will add at least an hour to our journey."

"No, it won't," Simon said, his tone firm and grim. "Because we're not doing it."

She gasped as she faced him again. "What are you talking about? If we don't do it, we won't get home."

"That's exactly right. We aren't getting home. Not right now." He squeezed her hand. "You're shivering, and if we trod all around the estate in this downpour for the next two hours, you're going to freeze. And honestly, so will I. But I have an idea of where to go." He smiled, and she noted the expression didn't reach his eyes.

"Where?" she asked.

He drew her forward and she trotted after him as he took them back where they'd come from, then veered them off the main path and through the wet and miserable woods.

"Simon, where are we going?" she asked again.

"The caretaker lodge," he said.

She wrinkled her brow. "God, I haven't even thought of that place in years. It's been empty since…I think Father was still alive when our last caretaker lived there. How do you even know about it?"

Simon winked over his shoulder at her and she nearly lost her footing at the cheeky expression on his wet face. "I know a great many things." He laughed, then said, "In truth, we used to come here when I'd visit. When your father was alive, James needed—"

"An escape," she whispered, completing the sentence as memories flooded her. She winced at them. "I needed one too."

Simon's hand tightened around hers. "I wish we'd brought you. Though I doubt you would have been very interested in duke talk and fishing."

"Fishing I would have been," she said, noticing that his pace was increasing. It was exhausting, but at least moving kept her a bit warmer. "I loved to fish."

"Well, next time we all run away from home, I'll be sure to invite you," he said.

She smiled, but said, "Next time you run away from home, Graham will be running away from *me*. I doubt he'll approve of my joining you."

At that Simon's posture stiffened and he didn't speak for the next five minutes that he dragged her through the woods. She was beginning to give up hope they'd find the place when they came through the canopy of trees, and there it was.

It wasn't much. Just a basic two-room cottage that had housed their old caretaker for decades. He had died and their father had not replaced him right away. Once James had taken over the estate, he'd built a far nicer one much closer to the house, since the current caretaker was married to their housekeeper. This old place had been abandoned years ago, and its boarded-up windows and the rusty hinges on the doors spoke to that.

But right now it was better than the finest palace.

Simon released her hand at last, fumbling under a rock by the door. He came up with a folded piece of cloth, which he unwrapped to reveal a key. He grinned at her as he fitted it in the lock and managed to wrestle the rickety door open.

He motioned her inside and she rushed past him, more grateful to be out of the rain than she had ever been for anything in her life. She stood in the very dark room, her eyes slowly adjusting, as Simon entered and then fought to get the creaky hinges moving to shut the door behind them.

There was a big fireplace in the main room with a settee covered in a dusty cloth, set on a thick rug. A small cupboard was in the back corner on the opposite side of the room and a table with just one chair. The door on the back wall was closed, but she assumed it led to the bedroom.

Simon reached out and she jumped as his hand closed over her forearm. In the close and the dark, he suddenly felt so big next to her. His presence seemed to suck the air out of the room.

The room where they were alone. No one would be coming for them in this mess of weather.

"God, James must be beside himself," she whispered.

Simon bent his head and his hand slipped from her arm. "I'm sure he is, but if he's noticed that I'm gone, as well, I hope he knows I would not let any harm befall you if I could prevent it. At any rate, if the rain stops we'll go back as soon as we can."

She nodded as a great shiver racked her. Now that they were not moving, the cold seemed to permeate her entire being.

He frowned. "I'll start a fire. I think I saw wood under the awning around the side of the house. It should be dry." He crossed the room and bent to clear out some of the old ash collected in the long-neglected fireplace. "You go into the bedroom and look for all the blankets you can find. Then undress."

She stared at him, unblinking, as shock washed over her. "Undress?" she repeated.

His gaze lifted and glittered in the dim light. "You'll freeze if you don't. We need to get your clothes dry, and they won't dry with you in them. So find a few blankets, wrap yourself up as best you can and leave your clothes in the bedroom by the fireplace in there."

She shifted. "But what about—"

He rose then, in one fluid movement, and reached out to catch her damp upper arms. That he touched her while he was talking to her about stripping out of her clothes made what he said all the more powerful. She caught her breath, her words screeching to a halt because she could no longer recall how to formulate them.

"Meg," he said, laughing a little, though she thought it might be a bit nervous of a laugh. "Until you are safe, I'm going to stay wet. And I'm cold. So for my sake, stop arguing and get undressed."

She worried her lip a bit and then nodded. "All right." She turned away from his touch and moved toward the bedroom in the back of the cottage. As she touched the dusty handle, she turned back toward him. "Simon?"

"Yes," he said, his tone filled with frustration that told her she wasn't moving fast enough.

"I'm—I'm sorry."

He stared at her a long moment, then motioned to the door. "Go on. We'll have plenty of time to talk once we're both warm."

She left him, her hands shaking, not just from the cold but from the notion that within moments she would be naked with him. Naked with the man she loved more than anything in this world.

And she had no idea what would happen next.

Simon stood in front of the fire that now glowed hot and bright in the main room of the cottage. It helped a little, but he was still wet to the bone and cold. Of course, he also had a cockstand that rubbed painfully against the front of his soaked trousers.

"That's a first," he muttered.

Cold and wet normally were not conducive to such a thing, but here he was. Hard as steel, listening to Meg get undressed through the thin wooden door. Just a tiny barrier between him and smooth skin, long legs, open arms that he could...

"No," he managed to remind himself through clenched teeth. "*No.*"

The door behind him opened at last and he forced himself to turn and look as Meg exited the bedroom. His mouth instantly went dry. She was wrapped in a thin gray blanket, in a rather poor toga style. Her hair was half down, tendrils of it teasing beneath the edge of the covering and pressing wet curls against all the skin that was exposed to him.

And there was so much skin. Most of her shoulders were bare, her back was bare, her neck was bare, as were the swell of her breasts that peeked up over the edge of the blanket. And then there was leg. So much smooth, glorious leg. The blanket only reached to just above her knee and he stared at those legs.

"Simon?" she said, her voice tense.

He forced his gaze back to her face. "Yes. Good."

She wrinkled her brow at his response and came farther into the room, toward the warmth of the fire. Toward him and his raging cockstand, which was now even worse, if that were to be believed.

"I-I left another blanket on the bed for you," she said.

He nodded and stepped back from her. His tone was sharp as he repeated, "Good."

He walked away without saying anything else, only pausing to grab the stack of wood he'd placed near the bedroom door so he could build a fire in there, as well.

He shut the door behind him, shut himself into almost pitch darkness and leaned back against it with a ragged sigh. There were tests in a man's life. He knew that, he'd encountered many. This was one, wasn't it? A test of control. Of loyalty.

He had to pass, that was all there was to it.

He set the logs down and went about making a quick fire. Once it had begun to glow, he stood before it, undressing. His hands kept brushing that unwanted erection and he grunted at the sensation.

He let his trousers fall, tugged his sopping wet shirt over his head and then took himself firmly in hand. The only way to make this better was to slake the need. So he stroked once, twice, leaning one hand against the mantel as he pictured going back into the main room, pressing Meg against the wall and lifting her onto him. Taking her with long, steady strokes until she shattered around him, whispering his name into his shoulder.

He came in pearly spurts, biting his lip to keep from crying out at the pleasure that coursed through his body. Once he was spent, he pressed his other hand to the mantel and leaned there with his full weight.

"Get yourself together," he cursed, hating himself for what he'd just done. What he still wanted to do.

He picked up all their wet clothes, wrung them in the cracked washbasin near the door and began to hang them. His went first, then her dress. His breath caught as he lifted her chemise. It was see-through thanks to the wetness. He shut his eyes as he draped it on the back of a chair and turned it to face the fire. Her stockings, silky and fine, went next to it, and then he wiped off his hands and gathered up the blanket.

It wasn't going to cover much, but he did his best, wrapping it around his waist like it was a kilt before he drew a long breath. He had to go back out there. He had to face Meg. He had to face his fantasies.

Right now.

He pushed the door open and caught his breath. She was bent over the fire, putting another log in to feed the massive flame. Her blanket had dipped in the process and he caught a glimpse of the side of her full, lush breast.

She straightened and turned as if sensing him there. Her breath caught and her gaze slipped down from his face to his bare chest. She just stood there, staring at him like he was staring at her, and everything in his world grew tight and focused.

Meg wanted him. He'd seen that before, but now it rose up, rushing toward him like an out of control phaeton. She wanted him and they were alone and no one would ever have to know.

"Graham," he muttered under his breath, trying hard to think of the man who he'd considered one of his best friends for so long.

She swallowed hard and motioned him closer, like a siren driving him toward rocks. "Come warm up," she said, her voice rough.

He moved to stand with her and they stared into the flames,

their bare arms nearly touching, but not quite. An almost perfect metaphor for their entire relationship, it seemed. Almost there, but not quite.

As if she read his thoughts she moved to face him. Her expression was taut with tension and her hands trembled at her sides. He held his breath, waiting for whatever she was going to say. It looked important. It looked life-changing. And he wasn't certain he was ready for it.

~

Everything Meg had ever wanted to say to this man sat on the tip of her tongue, ready to be confessed in the strange little world only they inhabited. But as she stared at him, at his tense face, at his gloriously handsome face, her nerve faltered.

What good was saying anything? It was evident that Simon wanted her, but he had made no attempt ever to act on that desire. Perhaps that meant it was nothing more than need, not love. If she said what she felt and he didn't truly care, he would think less of her. If he did care...well, that almost made it worse. They could never be together. James had guaranteed that by promising her to Graham all those years ago.

She swallowed her confessions back and whispered, "It's getting dark."

He glanced toward the boarded windows. Far less light was coming past the gaps now. "Part of that is the heaviness of the storm, but it's also getting late. We..." He hesitated and turned his face away from hers. "We might not make it back tonight, Meg."

She stiffened at that statement. She'd been so wrapped up in Simon all afternoon, she'd never considered not making it back a possibility. But now it loomed up, a crushing reality that had consequences. So many consequences.

"But...but if we don't make it back, people will...they'll know we are *both* missing," she whispered.

His mouth turned to a grim frown and he refused to look at her. "Yes. I'm certain our mutual disappearance has already been marked by more than just James and Emma."

She couldn't help but gasp. "They'll think—if we spend a night away alone together, they'll think—"

Simon bent his head even farther and his hands clenched against his thighs, outlined beneath the blanket. "Yes. They may think very ill of us, despite the circumstances," he admitted quietly. "But Graham will know better, won't he?"

He said Graham's name softly, almost like he was afraid of invoking him by saying it. She shivered as she thought of her fiancé, thought of what he'd say when she returned.

"In truth, I…" she began, then stopped. But as she stared at Simon, his outline in the firelight, she knew honesty was where they would end up tonight. It was too hard to pretend with him, the man who knew her most and best. "I hardly know Graham at all."

His gaze jerked to her and she couldn't tell if that statement surprised him or made him angry. "What do you mean?" he snapped. "You've been engaged for years, Meg. Of course you know him."

She nodded. "So many years. And yet he isn't my friend. Not like you."

He turned toward her, leaning in, and her heart almost stopped. He looked like he wanted to touch her, and she found herself lifting her face toward his in readiness for the moment she'd been waiting for all her life.

But he turned away instead and moved toward the opposite side of the room. "I'll look for food," he murmured over his shoulder.

Meg moved toward the settee that he had apparently uncovered after he built the fire earlier and took a place on it, covering her face with her hands. She was trembling, and it wasn't from the cold. She wasn't certain she would survive this.

She wasn't sure she wanted to.

CHAPTER 5

I t was slim pickings, but a packet of dried fruit Simon assured her had been brought to the cottage by James and the other men just a few months ago and a bottle of wine would tide them over. It wasn't as if they were going to stay here forever. Simon almost laughed at that thought, though there was nothing funny about this situation. If they were going to stay here forever, never go back to the consequences, Simon knew exactly what he'd do. And it would have *nothing* to do with food or honor.

Meg shifted in her place at the table and adjusted her ever-sliding blanket. It was fascinating to watch it move over her skin, and yet he forced himself to look away. These wayward thoughts were entirely too dangerous in their current situation. If he wasn't careful, he was going to lose all reason and do something rash that could never be taken back.

The room was utterly quiet, and Meg looked upward, drawing his attention to the banging of the rain on the roof. It had eased up slightly from the torrent it had begun as hours before, but it was still far too hard to consider making a run back to the house on foot. Especially in the increasing darkness outside.

"It's not going to stop, is it?" she asked, her voice thin and her face pale in the candlelight.

He swallowed at that question. It could fit so many things about this situation, but she meant the rain. He had to focus.

"No, I don't think we'll see it let up any time soon, considering it's been doing this for almost two hours."

She bent her head. They *both* knew the consequences of what had happened here. They would spend a night together, unsupervised. The talk when they returned to James's estate would be vicious and instantaneous. Probably it was already happening amongst the party guests.

Because of that, Meg and Graham would likely have to marry right away after this. If she had a child any time in the next year, people would whisper that it could be Simon's, even though that would not be possible.

A child. Simon gritted his teeth. The idea of her having a child with Graham was the thing he most often tried to avoid when he thought of her future. Of course, it would happen eventually. Northridge needed heirs and spares to carry on his title, just as they all did. Graham and Meg would probably have a huge family in the end. How could he resist her, after all, once he'd had a chance to touch her?

Simon's stomach turned.

"What do we do?" she asked.

The resignation to her tone cut him to his very bone, and there was nothing he could do to console her. Especially not with his body on edge like this.

He sighed. "Go to bed," he suggested. "We'll go to sleep and wake up early and hopefully be able to make our way back through dryer elements."

She lifted her gaze to his and her body let out a great shiver. He frowned. Despite the blankets and the fire, she was still cold. Come to think of it, so was he. And with night descending it was only going to get worse in the drafty cottage.

He stood up and looked down at her. He was about to suggest something that was likely the worst idea he'd ever had. Something he wasn't completely certain was for her own good or his satisfaction. Something ungentlemanly no matter how much he tried to tell himself otherwise. If she slapped him across the face, he would deserve it. And yet he was still going to say it.

He *needed* to say it.

"Meg, the best way to fight a chill like this is…body heat," he managed to force out past suddenly very dry lips. "Would you be… opposed…to sharing the bed? For the purposes of increasing warmth only."

Her mouth opened in shock and he saw a dozen emotions cross her face. One was most definitely the kind of interest that an unmarried lady would do well to deny. He tried to ignore that interest and gritted his teeth as he waited for her to process the request.

"But we're…*naked*. Our clothes won't be dry for—"

"Hours, yes," he agreed. "We can't put them back on until morning, probably, or risk getting even colder."

She swallowed. "So we would lay *naked* together in a bed."

When she said it like that, it slammed Simon up short. "Yes," he whispered. "But I promise you Meg, I wouldn't do anything untoward. As soon as morning came, I would leave you. We will go home and there is no reason in the world that anyone would ever have to know what happened here. I'll tell your brother and Graham that I slept in the outer hall and that you took the bed. I'll even tell them that you leaned a chair against the door to protect your chastity."

"You would lie," she said.

He shrugged. "I would protect your future."

She turned her face at that statement. "It would be our secret," she said, still soft and her tone as unreadable as to her thoughts.

He nodded slowly. "Yes."

"And you are certain it will help with warmth?"

"It will," he said swiftly, for that, at least, was true even if the remainder of his motives were suspect.

She stood. "Then we should do it. I can see you're cold—you stayed in wet clothing far longer than I did. I would rather have this secret and not get sick or freeze than mince and mewl and protect myself from you, someone I trust implicitly."

Simon swallowed back a strangled groan. If she knew the wicked things in his heart, she would not trust him. No one would trust him. He hardly trusted himself.

But he smiled at her and motioned for the bedroom. "You go in and get yourself situated under the blankets so I won't...see anything. I'll stoke the fire out here and join you in a moment."

She gave him one last lingering look and then slipped past him and into the bedroom, where she shut the door behind her. When she was gone, he let out a long, heavy breath.

This was a terrible idea. Terrible. And yet everything in him thrilled at the idea of this one stolen night with Meg.

M eg watched as Simon leaned over the fire in the bedroom and stoked the flames as high as they would go, sending a bright glow into the small room. He took the time to adjust their drying clothing, turning each item and moving the chairs and pieces to different hooks. When he touched her chemise or her stockings, she jolted with the intimacy of that action.

When he was done, he faced her at last, and she caught her breath.

In the firelight, with that blanket riding low on his hips and his bare chest so perfectly muscled, he was beautiful. So beautiful he almost didn't seem real anymore. But then he never had been fully real, in a way.

Simon had always been her fantasy man, brought to life in physical form. A man with mischievousness and fun, intelligence and strength, confidence and competence. She had spun him up to be almost perfect, so much so that whenever they'd been apart, she'd told herself that her memory couldn't be right. But then they'd meet again and there he was: perfect.

Perfect for her.

Except that he was forever out of reach. At first because she'd been far too young for him to consider. Then because James had set her marriage to Graham, ending all possibility of a different life or future.

But tonight Simon moved toward her and she could almost pretend this was their wedding night. That he was hers and tonight he would make her his. Her body reacted to that fantasy, her nipples abraded by the rough blanket and her thighs getting wet with excitement she should not feel.

He turned his back to her, and she supposed she was meant to close her eyes. She did so, but only partially, still wickedly watching him as he dropped the blanket around his waist and added it on top of the covers that would protect them from the outside temperatures. Her mouth went totally dry as she stared at his muscular backside, his strong thighs. Then he turned and she almost gasped out loud and gave away her naughty observation of him. His member—she knew men called it a cock—was...well, it was very large and it appeared to be semi-hard. How he roamed about in the world with that thing between his legs, she did not understand.

He pulled the blankets back and she squeezed her eyes shut the rest of the way as he moved himself into position next to her. The bed was narrow, only barely fitting two people, and their arms touched as he settled into place on the flat pillow.

"Good night, Meg," he said, his voice rough and low beside her.

"Good night, Simon," she whispered back as she stared up at the ceiling.

They lay like that for she didn't know how long. It could have only been moments, but it felt like hours. She was so fully aware of the brush of his arm against hers. The weight of his body on the uncomfortable mattress. The sound of his breathing in the silence of the room.

Her mind spun on all of it, wildly out of control. No matter how much she wanted it, this night should *not* have happened. And Simon would likely suffer for it more than she would. Oh, people would whisper and hiss and she might lose some friends who judged her or called her a wanton without any basis for such censor. But once she married Graham, people's memory of this mistake would fade.

But for Simon, the effects would likely go on longer. And she could imagine James and Graham would not be happy with him. She would protest their judgment, of course, but would it matter? She could well picture James telling Simon he shouldn't have followed her at all or should have taken a horse to get back sooner or should have, should have, should have…

Her upset, created during the party when she'd seen Simon and Graham standing together—the future that had been thrust upon her and the one she would never have—had caused a great deal of problems now. And for the one person she would never have hurt in this world.

She rolled slowly, facing him in the dark. "Simon?" she whispered.

There was no answer. His face was turned slightly, so she couldn't tell if his eyes were closed or open.

"Simon?" she repeated, this time with less certainty.

"What?" he responded, his voice tight.

"I-I'm sorry I ruined today," she said slowly. "I'm sorry I caused all this trouble by running off from the party."

He didn't say anything, but he shifted just a little. His shoulders relaxed a fraction. She took that as the encouragement he didn't say out loud and continued.

"I feel like I should explain myself," she said with a sigh. The darkness, the intimacy of lying in a bed together, it all made it seem safe to say what was in her heart. Not all of it, of course. But some. If Simon understood, then perhaps this would be easier, somehow. "I-I don't want to marry *him*."

There, the words were out. Words she had never spoken to any other soul. She'd somehow expected when she said them for them to lose some of their rotting power. But instead, it made her anxiety about her future all the stronger.

"Meg..." Simon said, his tone a warning.

But she was past warnings now. Now the words seemed to fall from her lips even if she didn't want them to. "It isn't that I don't like Graham, or that he isn't a fine match. God knows he is a fine match—any woman would fight to be in my place. But that doesn't change the facts. And the fact is that there isn't a connection between us."

"Meg," Simon said again, this time with more urgency.

"Not the connection that there is when I'm with—"

Simon rolled unexpectedly, pushing her onto her back on the mattress, his hands coming to grip her upper arms as he loomed over her, his body covering half of hers as he stared down into her face with wild eyes. Her jovial, playful friend Simon was not there in this man's face that was so close to her own. He had been replaced by a dark, hard, passionate Simon who held her down and made her body ache even more with a wanting that was wrong and right all at the same time.

"Stop," he hissed. "Don't say another word, Margaret, or I'll —I'll—"

What little breath she had left in her lungs caught in her throat. "What? What will you do?" she asked.

He groaned deep in the back of his throat and then his mouth crushed down on hers. Simon was kissing her. The shock of that was so powerful she didn't think to fight it.

His grip loosened on her arms and she lifted them up, wrapping them around his neck and drawing him closer as relief flooded her.

It was like a dam had been broken, one built from years and years of stolen glances and hidden longing. Now everything she'd ever felt or wanted from this man was cascading over her and she was lost to its power. To *his* power.

His mouth was rough on hers, opening so his tongue could push inside her. She allowed it, meeting the kiss with her own, unpracticed, yes, but just as passionate. He stroked her tongue, seeming to taste every inch of her as his weight pushed her into the pillows. She was beginning to understand and did the same to him, eliciting another soft groan from him.

His hands moved, too, sliding down her bare sides, gripping her hips in the darkness beneath the blankets and pushing himself against her. She lifted to his weight, gasping when the hard cock she'd seen earlier thrust against her lower belly, insistent and hot.

"Simon," she gasped into his mouth, overwhelmed by pleasure and need all at once. It was all so heady and dangerous and wanton and wonderful.

He froze at the sound of his name, his hands stilling, his mouth stopping. Then he released her in an instant and jumped off of her as quickly as he could. He caught the blanket on top and wrapped it around himself as he paced away to the fire.

"No!" he shouted, loud enough that the room almost shook. She thought that the exclamation was as much to himself as to her, and she winced at the pain in that one little word.

"No," he repeated, and there was even more pain in the softer admonishment.

He moved toward the door and she sat up, the blankets sliding from her breasts as she did so, but she didn't care.

"Where are you going?" she asked. "Please, Simon."

"I can't, Meg," he said, spinning to face her. He stared, and she blushed before she covered herself. "I *can't*, don't you see? No matter how I want to, no matter how I *need* to. He is one of my closest friends. Practically a brother when I had no one else in the world.

They *both* are. I'm sleeping on the floor. I should have done so to begin with."

Her lips parted. "But the cold—"

"Then I'll freeze," he snapped, exiting the room and slamming the door behind himself.

She flopped back on the bed, covering her face with her forearm as the tears began to fall.

CHAPTER 6

S imon shifted and grunted as pain shot up his arm. Every part
of his body felt stiff and bruised. He remained with his eyes
closed, caught between restless sleep and wakefulness, and tried to
remember exactly why everything felt so awful.

And then he heard the voices. Distant, through glass and wood,
but there. He recognized those voices. James saying, "—one of the
few people to know where this place is."

Then Graham, his tone angry. "—at least it would protect her."

Simon shot to his feet, all the memories of last night coming
cascading down on him. He and Meg caught in the storm. He and
Meg, lying in that bed together. Kissing Meg and having it be so
much better than anything he'd ever dreamed.

And so much worse.

He'd had every intention of waking her early, of them being fully
dressed before dawn. But thanks to that searing kiss, he'd hardly
slept, probably less than an hour, and clearly most of that hour had
been recent.

Now Graham and James and…there was another voice, one he
didn't recognize. Well, *they* were here. And he was naked except for

a blanket, and all his clothes were in a bedroom with Meg, equally naked.

"Shit!" he burst out, tucking the blanket around himself just as the door began to open.

"It's unlocked!" he heard James say, relief in his voice as the door swung fully open and revealed James, Graham and the Viscount Baxton, a distant friend of their group. Also one of the most gossipy gentleman in Society. All three of them stopped and stared as they saw Simon standing in his little blanket and nothing else.

Graham's eyes narrowed and Lord Baxton's widened. James stepped forward, his expression uncertain. "Thank God, Simon. We were worried sick. Is Meg with you?"

"Yes," Simon said slowly. "We were caught out in the storm. I had to bring her here, she was soaked to the bone and—"

Before he could finish, the bedroom door opened and all the men pivoted to face it as Meg stepped into the main hall. Simon's eyes fluttered shut. She was still wearing only the blanket and her hair was mussed from sleep. She looked gorgeous as ever, but she also looked…well-loved.

She caught her breath, tugging her blanket up higher, and her gaze flickered to Simon.

There was a beat of a moment where everyone was silent, staring at each other, the meaning of all this sinking in for each person.

Then Graham lunged forward. "You son of a bitch!" he bellowed before he swung and punched Simon square in the nose.

~

Meg screamed as Simon staggered beneath the force of Graham's blow, nearly falling onto the settee. Blood began to trickle from his nose, but Graham didn't look finished either as he took a long step forward.

She didn't think. She just moved, rushing to lodge herself

between the men. "No, stop! Please, Graham, stop!" she said, blocking Simon as she clutched at her blanket with one hand and pushed Graham back with the other.

He stared down at her, his gaze suddenly very focused. And very angry. She'd never seen him so angry, or so *anything* emotional, in all the time they had been engaged.

"What is this, Margaret?" Graham hissed, his gaze holding hers, forcing her not to look away, telling her everything he thought of her. "*This* is what you're doing?"

"I've done nothing," she said, lifting her chin and trying not to think of that kiss with Simon. "We were trapped, that is all. I have done nothing wrong."

Graham let out a bark of angry laughter. "It doesn't look that way to me. It looks like you opened your—"

Now it was Simon who lunged from behind her. "You shut your goddamned mouth and have some respect!" he shouted, his hand coming to settle on Meg's back.

She appreciated the protection, but since every single man in the room tracked the inappropriate movement of his hand, it didn't help their situation.

James stepped forward, catching Graham's arms as Meg pushed back at Simon to hold him from the fight. "Enough!" James snapped, his sharp tone silencing the room. He shoved Graham toward Baxton. "Get him out of here. You two ride back to the estate and I will deal with you there."

Graham shook his head. "There is no *dealing*, James. Is there? Is there, Simon?"

James glared at him and sent a side glance to Baxton, who was barely containing his grin of glee at the drama unfolding. Meg held back a sob. What a tale he would have to tell.

"Go. Back. Home," James said.

Baxton at last took Graham's arm and tugged him out the door, with Graham sending looks of pure rage at Simon the entire time.

Once they had left, James slammed the door behind them and turned to Simon and Meg.

Meg had seen her brother through many a troubling scenario. Through their father's abuse and neglect, through their mother's many outbursts when she was drunk, through his courtship with Emma, which had not been entirely smooth. Today, looking at her, he had an expression she had never seen before. There was tension on his face, worry, anger and a touch of what she knew was disappointment.

She had disappointed him, and that cut her all the way down through her heart. She turned away from it, blinking at the tears that rushed to her eyes.

"Go into the bedroom and get dressed, Meg," James said softly. "Simon will do the same out here."

Simon cleared his throat. "Er, my clothes are in the other room."

James jerked his face toward Simon, and the disappointment Meg had seen directed at her was tripled for him. "Of course they are," James growled. "Margaret, bring the Duke of Crestwood's things to me and I will deliver them. Then get dressed in the bedroom. *Please.*"

"Yes, Jamie," Meg whispered, reverting to her childhood nickname for him in the hopes it would soften him to her.

He said nothing as she entered the room and caught up all of Simon's clothing. She brought them back and handed them over to James. He touched her hand once he held everything, then wordlessly leaned forward to kiss her cheek.

"Can you manage?"

She nodded and looked over his shoulder one last time at Simon. He was staring at her, his expression filled with guilt and regret. Regret over what they'd shared. She supposed she should feel the same, considering what their actions had now wrought.

But she didn't. And seeing those emotions on his face broke her heart anew. Slowly, she closed the door and covered her face. Her entire world had just broken. It was very likely nothing could fix any of it.

~

James threw the clothing and Simon barely caught it as it hit his chest with enough force that it nearly took the air out of him. They stood there, staring at each other for a long moment before the silence was broken by the sound of three gunshots in the distance.

"What was that?" Simon asked.

James shook his head, his dark eyes snapping with emotion. "*That* is Baxton firing off shots to tell all the others searching for you that you and Meg have been found safe."

Simon swallowed. "All the others?"

"Yes. All our friends and most of the other men in our party spread out all over the estate at dawn this morning, hoping to find you and my sister alive."

Simon bent his head, trying not to think about the frantic, terrible night James must have endured. The love he felt for his sister was deep and strong after the childhood they had gone through together. Even a hint that she might be lost to him must have choked James with fear.

"What the bloody hell were you thinking, Simon?" James hissed.

Simon sighed as he tugged his trousers on and let the blanket fall away at last. He shook out his shirt as he pondered the right answer to the question. The truth seemed the only way out.

But not all of it.

"I wasn't *thinking* at all," he admitted. "I saw Meg sneak away from the party. She was obviously upset about something, so I followed her."

"That wasn't your place," James ground out.

Simon hesitated. No, it was not. And he'd known it when he did it. He'd gone anyway. And he hadn't stopped her until they were far away from the house, until the storm was looming...perhaps there was part of him that had orchestrated all this.

Which made it all the worse.

"I- I wasn't lying when I said we got caught out in the storm. Nor was *she* lying when she told you that nothing...nothing happened between us."

His mind ripped him back to that kiss in the bed. To her soft, naked body trapped against his as she sighed and moaned into his mouth. That moment when he had almost lost control and driven himself into her so no one else could ever lay claim to her.

But he hadn't. Somehow he hadn't.

"I should call you out if Graham won't," James said, shaking his head as he paced the small room. "Naked together in this tiny place?"

"What was I to do, let her freeze to death in her wet clothing in order to maintain some decorum?" Simon asked, glaring at James before he at last tugged his shirt on and began buttoning it.

"No." James pressed his lips together hard. "Of course not."

"Look, if either of you decide to call me out, it will be entirely understandable." Simon sighed. "I would not deny you that pleasure. I *deserve* the consequences of my actions."

"Of your feelings?" James clarified, facing him and spearing him with a glare.

Simon lifted his chin. "Perhaps those, too." James's eyes went wide as he stared, unspeaking, at Simon for what felt like an eternity. "You never wanted me for her. You loved Graham more, and I may have...I *have*...ruined that."

James's forehead wrinkled in what seemed like genuine shock. "Loved Graham more? Is *that* what you really think?"

"That is what is true," Simon said softly. "I accepted that years ago, James."

Which wasn't exactly true. The fact that James wanted Graham as his true brother still stung occasionally. But not as much as losing Meg did.

"I chose Graham because you were still whoring around half of London at the time," James said, raising his hands as if in surrender. "Great God, you and Roseford fucked women together from time to time, if I remember the drunken bragging correctly."

Simon flinched. "Robert bragged. I did not."

"Either way, you weren't ready to settle down. I didn't think you'd be open to the idea of an engagement. But Simon, look at me."

Simon lifted his stare from the dusty wooden floor he'd been focusing on and made himself look at James. James's face was softer now. The anger and disappointment were still there, but there was something strong above it all.

"What?" Simon asked.

"Not choosing you was never about a lack of love for you," James said.

Simon nodded and a weight was lifted from his shoulders. Of course, another had already settled there and it was far heavier than the first. As if James read his mind, his mouth tugged down into a grim line.

"You know what has to happen now, I think."

Simon caught his breath. The moment the three men had burst into the room, he'd known what would happen. If it had only been Graham and James to find them, perhaps it would have been different.

But it wasn't. Baxton had been there, he had seen everything. Simon hadn't fully allowed himself to process what that meant, but now it was unavoidable.

"Yes," he whispered. "I'm going to have to marry her."

Meg fussed with her buttons and blinked at the tears that threatened to fall. She knew it was wrong to leave the door open a crack and listen to them, but she had done it anyway. At least until she heard too much and she'd backed away and dressed.

She'd heard James yell at Simon about whoring through London. About…sharing women with the Duke of Roseford. That was when she'd moved away. The idea of that was very confusing to her, for she didn't understand the logistics, but the meaning stung her. All the while that she had been pining for Simon, he had been moving from woman to woman, not even thinking about her?

Was she just another in that line? Was his kiss last night about her being just another warm body that he couldn't resist? Was everything she thought was between them just a lie?

She shook her head. It didn't really matter anymore. She had bigger problems out in front of her. A gossip who would spread this tale. A fiancé whose rage was palpable and completely understandable. The disappointment of a most-beloved brother. Those things were what she had to focus on.

Simon would have to take care of himself.

She took a long breath, then left the room. The two men stopped talking as soon as she stepped out, and she found herself looking at Simon even though she was trying not to do just that.

He was wrinkled and disheveled and his hair stuck up at odd angles. But he was perfect and beautiful, and her mind spun on the feel of his full lips on hers.

"Meg?" James stepped toward her and she pushed the other thoughts from her mind. His expression was gentler now than it had been when she entered the bedroom. He touched her cheek. "It's going to be all right."

Those words, those lies, broke her and she stepped into his arms. He smoothed his hands along her back as she said, "No. No, it won't be. I know it can't be. Not for a long time."

He let her shake in his arms for a moment before he drew back and smiled at her. "We will work this out, Meg. I promise you, and you know I never break my promises. Now, come. Emma has been worried sick. There is a carriage just through the woods on the road, and you and I will ride back to the estate together in it."

"A carriage?" she repeated in confusion. "Why a carriage?"

Some of the color left James's face. "Each search party took a carriage just in case someone found you...*hurt* and the vehicle was needed to rush you to a doctor."

Meg's lips parted as she stared at her brother's ashen face. "Oh, Jamie."

He shook his head. "You are well. Both of you. That is all that matters now."

She glanced over her shoulder. Simon was following them outside, silent and grim. "What about Simon? Will he ride in the carriage with us?"

"No, Simon will ride my horse back," James said, sending him a pointed look. "He needs air to clear his head."

Simon jerked out a swift nod, but still he was silent. It was amazing how much that silence meant. Usually Simon was the first to crack a joke and lighten the mood. There was nothing jovial on his face now. It was like he was another person.

Just as he had been right before he kissed her.

James took her arm and led her from the cottage. As they passed by Simon, she hesitated. "I-I'm so sorry," she whispered.

She expected, hoped, that he would respond to her. But he merely inclined his head and watched her go. Outside it was a bright and sunny morning, and she flinched at the stark light of it. James's horse was standing before the door and Simon caught the reins and led it through the woods until they reached the road. There a carriage awaited, driven by a servant who did not look at her as James opened the carriage door.

Simon looked, though. He watched as James helped her up into the carriage. The last glance she had was of him watching their vehicle drive away. She flopped back against the seat, closing her eyes briefly as she prepared for the lecture James was sure to give.

But he didn't. In fact, he didn't speak for almost ten full minutes, but let her sit, bombarded by her own thoughts and fears and memories.

Finally, he cleared his throat. "I may have made a mistake, arranging a marriage without consulting you."

Slowly she opened her eyes and looked at her brother. James was leaning forward, his elbows draped across his knees, his face drawn and taut.

This was a subject they had never addressed. What could she say once the deed was done, after all? But now he had opened the door, most unexpectedly, and she decided to take a deep breath and walk through it.

"Why did you?" she asked, thinking back to the blunt words between James and Simon earlier. James's accusations about Simon's behavior. She flinched.

He ran a hand through his hair. "God, Meg, I was so new at being duke. I worried every moment of every day that I'd fail."

"Like Father claimed you would," she whispered, reaching across to take his hand.

He nodded and the pain of the past flitted across his face. She had not seen that reflection in months. His relationship with Emma had tempered it greatly.

"I didn't care if I cocked it up for myself," he continued. "At that point, I was ready to run the title into the ground just to destroy the only thing that bastard ever truly loved. But I had you to think of. If I failed, you would be hurt, even destroyed. I didn't want that. A marriage..." He trailed off.

She sighed, for she understood what he didn't say. "A marriage would keep me safe. Especially one to a powerful duke. An old friend."

"That was exactly my thinking. I was so wrapped up in how it would help you that I didn't ever think of the harm it might do."

She ignored that statement for a moment and examined him closely. "And why did you pick Graham rather than Simon? Or any of your other friends, for that matter. You certainly had a plethora of dukes to pick from in your arrangements."

"A gaggle," he said with a soft smile. "Emma says a group of dukes is a gaggle."

She grinned despite the situation. "Well, Emma is always right. But I want to know the answer to my question."

He nodded. "You deserve it. I never considered anyone but Simon or Graham when the idea struck me. We were the closest of our group. But Simon—" He stopped and she froze, knowing he was thinking of the things he had said. Things he wouldn't say to her out of respect for her innocence.

"What?" she pressed, wanting to hear him say those things.

But he didn't. "I thought Graham would be the steadier choice." He looked out the window, and she could see they were almost back to the house now. Without the rain and with his best mounts leading the carriages, it was a much quicker return. "Meg, I'm so very sorry."

"Oh Jamie, I know you only ever wanted what was best for me," she whispered, tears escaping when she tried to hold them back. "And I should have told you a long time ago that I-I—"

He pressed his lips together. "Are you in love with Simon?"

She nodded, relieved she didn't have to say those words to him. She searched his face, looking for his disappointment or his censure. But there was none. He only looked heartbroken. For her. But also for the friendships that had been destroyed in one stormy night.

She had done that.

The carriage stopped and James reached out to wipe a tear from her cheek. "Well, my dearest, you may get your wish and have Simon."

Her eyes widened. "What do you mean?"

He leaned back and stared at her. "If it were only us, our friends, who found you...but we weren't. Baxton and Graham rode back ahead, and the viscount has probably already started spreading the worst version of what was seen today at the cottage. It is so big a scandal—"

Her lips parted. "Graham will not want to continue the engagement. Not that I can blame him. He was so very angry."

James nodded. "It is the betrayal, I think. Simon's."

She bent her head. The idea that her engagement to Graham would end and that she might end up with Simon instead had long been a dream of hers. But now it was a nightmare because of the actions that had brought them here.

"Oh God, James, the cost."

He smiled, trying to be reassuring, she thought, but failing. "We will have plenty of time to count the cost, Meg," he said as the carriage door opened and he stepped down. He reached back in to help her and squeezed her hand gently as she gave it to him. "For now, come. There will be a gauntlet. Your disappearance with Simon was quite the talk last night. I would not be surprised if most of the house is not up to wait to see what the outcome will be. Baxton and Graham's return will have only made that worse."

She lifted her chin as she exited the vehicle, and as she cast her gaze up to the house she found James's warning was a prescient one. Almost every window that overlooked the drive had a face peering from it.

Her heart sank as she took her brother's arm and let him lead her up the stairs. As they entered the foyer, she jolted. Emma was waiting there, and her pale face lit up as she rushed to embrace Meg.

"We were so worried," Emma whispered close to her ear.

"I'm sorry," Meg all but sobbed. "I'm so, so sorry."

"Hush," Emma reassured her, wrapping an arm around her and drawing her close.

She lifted her gaze to James and he leaned in to kiss his wife's cheek. Meg saw the unspoken communication between them. Felt her brother relax a fraction just from being in Emma's presence.

"How bad?" he said softly.

Emma pursed her lips. "Bad enough. Made worse when Baxton and Graham returned. Baxton went straight to the largest group of people to whisper what he saw. Graham went straight to your office, and judging from the crashing, I assume he has destroyed most of your glassware."

James flinched, as did Meg. Before either could respond, Simon came through the door. Emma smiled at him as Meg stared. His nose was still red and his expression was empty.

"Hello, Simon," Emma said softly. "I'm so glad you're safe. Thank you for keeping Meg safe, as well."

Simon seemed surprised, but he inclined his head. "I'm sorry to cause so much trouble, Emma."

She shrugged. "Trouble will come and go. That is the way of the world."

James glanced over his shoulder toward the hall that led to his office. "Graham will want an accounting."

Emma lifted her eyebrows. "I assume he will. But he can wait for it. I'm taking Meg upstairs to change. I think Simon should do the same. If you want to tell him he'll be joined in an hour, I think that would be best."

James pondered that. "I'll tell him. And if he gives me trouble, I'm sending for you."

"If he gives you trouble," Emma said as she took Meg's hand and started up the stairs with her, "he won't want *me* to come in. Be sure he understands that."

James stared up at her, his expression pure love as he called out, "I will."

Meg smiled at their connection. Her brother deserved nothing less than the love he had found with her friend. But in that moment, it only made her situation more stark. For when she looked at Simon, he didn't return her stare. He stayed at the bottom of the stairs, and it felt like she was leaving for far more than a mere moment.

It felt like this was a forever kind of goodbye.

CHAPTER 7

Almost an hour after his return to the house, Simon was bathed and shaved, and now he stood in front of the mirror, his valet smoothing his waistcoat of all wrinkles and straightening the already perfect knot of his cravat.

"The black jacket?" Swanson asked as he stepped away and lifted his choice for judgment.

"Why not? It matches the bruises," Simon said, staring at his reflection.

Since his return to the house, his nose had swollen and dark bruises were beginning to spread up to his eyes. They were a clear indication that it was broken from Graham's well-placed punch earlier in the day. *That* would certainly not help with the talk around the party, but there wasn't much he could do about it now.

Aside from the broken nose, Simon felt he looked well put together. He would need to be. He was about to face a firing squad. And once it was over, he would likely be hastened into a quick marriage.

A fact he didn't want to thrill at. He shouldn't. He didn't *deserve* to be happy over this stolen future with Meg when he had caused such heartache to people he'd called his brothers for decades. When he had caused such damage to her.

As Swanson slid the jacket over his shoulders, there was a sudden pounding at the door. Both men turned toward the sound, and Simon's heart sank. No servant would bang so loudly, nor would James if he'd simply come to check on Simon's progress before the final showdown.

Which left only one option for the person behind the door.

"Let him in," he said to Swanson. "And then you may go."

His valet looked uncertain, but didn't argue the point as he moved to the door and opened it to reveal Graham standing outside. Simon shifted his shoulders back and forced himself to meet his friend's eyes as Swanson edged past, his expression filled with worry at the tension that now coursed between the men.

"Come in," Simon said when Graham didn't move.

Graham's eyebrow arched. "Inviting me inside like nothing happened?"

Simon drew a sharp breath at the cold, hard quality of Graham's tone. He fought to keep his own neutral. "No, there's no way I can look into the mirror and not know what happened earlier."

"You want me to apologize for breaking your pretty face?" Graham drawled.

"No. I want you to come inside because there are likely a dozen listening ears in the hallway," Simon said through clenched teeth. "And I think whatever you have to say requires privacy."

"Privacy. Yes, you'd know all about that, wouldn't you? What you did last night with my fiancée required privacy, didn't it? And you bloody well arranged a situation where you'd have it," Graham hissed as he came inside the room and slammed the door behind him, hard enough that one of the portraits on the wall fell clattering to the wooden floor.

Neither man moved to retrieve it, but they stood staring at each other. Simon struggled to find words to say to Graham, but it was almost impossible. His friend's words were true, at least to some extent. Simon hated himself for it.

"You're angry, Graham," Simon said softly. "And you have every right to be. I'm not making excuses for what I did last night. For what you stumbled upon this morning."

Graham laughed, but it was a hard, angry sound that crackled through the room. "But?"

Simon clenched his fists at his sides. "Nothing happened," he said. "*Nothing* happened. You must know me well enough to trust me when I tell you that, looking into your eyes."

Graham shook his head slowly. "I think it may be that I didn't know you at all. Nor her, it seems."

Simon stiffened. "If you want to be angry at me, slander me, go ahead. I deserve it, I can take it. But *stop* including her in this. Meg was not at fault."

"You two," Graham breathed. "Always thick as thieves. Always turning toward each other, whispering and giggling, *dancing*."

Simon clenched his jaw. "You don't like to dance, Meg does. It's the only reason—"

"Clearly not the *only* reason," Graham interrupted.

Simon bent his head. "I suppose not."

"James came in to talk to me. To say that you two needed to tidy up after your dirty little night together and that I had to wait for my satisfaction. He's trying to make me feel better, you see, by telling me he believes there have been feelings between you for years."

Simon flinched. "I wish he had let me tell you that myself. And why aren't you still with him? I can't imagine he sent you up here to have this conversation while you're in this mindset."

"He didn't," Graham conceded. "He went to talk to Baxton. Apparently the viscount is spreading the story around the entire party. I don't know why James is bothering to put a stop to him. Once Baxton said that kind of gossip out loud, there was no way it wasn't going to spread like wildfire."

"No," Simon whispered, hating himself. "It's too good."

Graham tilted his head and looked at Simon closer. "It *is*, isn't it? After all, how often do two dukes, friends since they were children, fight over another duke's sister? How often does one of those dukes and said sister slide behind the other's back and...what did you tell me? Do *nothing* together. Do nothing while naked."

Simon gritted his teeth harder. Graham was spoiling for a fight and he was baiting Simon now, saying everything he could to make Simon start it. And it was working, for Simon was starting to want nothing more than to return the punch that had broken his nose earlier.

"Stop, please," he whispered.

Graham shook his head. "Did you laugh at me while you did *nothing* with my fiancée? Were you planning on telling me all along, bragging like you used to do with all the women you fucked over the years? Or were you two going to keep it quiet, let her marry me and just continue to carry on behind my back?"

Simon lunged then, pushed to his limit and beyond. He caught Graham's lapels and slammed him back, smashing him against the wall with all his strength.

"I would never have done that, goddamn it, Graham. You should know better. I was going to leave. Roseford and I were leaving in a day or two, out of the country, and I wasn't going to come back, not until after you were married. What happened last night wasn't some way to get over on you."

"Even though you have feelings for her?" Graham asked, not fighting Simon's grip. Not moving at all except to look down at him, his gaze steady and unwavering.

"Yes," Simon whispered. "Yes, I have feelings for her. I have had feelings for her for almost a decade. And I *never* acted on them, I never acted on them once, because of you. But you can't act like you care this much, damn you. You don't want her, you never did. And here I was, dying inside knowing that she would be yours. That you would one day touch her like I wanted to, that you would one day have children with her that I would have to look at, see her eyes and your hair. *You didn't want her*, Graham. And I did."

"My problem isn't that you wanted her," Graham growled. "My problem is that if you'd told me a year ago or five years ago, I would have stepped aside and wished you nothing but happiness. But you *didn't* tell me. You let it fester, you let it change our friendship over the past half a decade. A friendship that you claim means so much to you. And then you reached out and you stole her from me in the most public way you could muster."

Simon drew back, releasing Graham's lapels and turning away toward the fire. He didn't know what to say to that charge. There was nothing *to* say, really. Whatever his intentions, whatever his goals, he had done exactly what Graham said.

"You are my friend, Graham," he said softly. "I never would have hurt you on purpose."

Graham moved toward him, his eyes narrowed. "You were *never* my friend, Simon. And you did." He passed by to the door and paused there. "Now let's go downstairs. There are things to be done. Humiliations to be made complete. You have a bride to finish winning and I want to get on with it so I can go home."

He opened the door and Simon squeezed his eyes shut at the sound of a half a dozen footsteps scurrying away. Eavesdroppers, whisperers who would multiply this story, magnify it.

All of them would suffer for it: Graham, Meg, Emma, James... though only Simon deserved the censure and gossip. He opened his eyes and watched Graham walk away without so much as a backward glance. It killed him to do it, for he knew what that moment meant.

He had just lost one of his dearest friends. His life would never be the same.

~

E mma had turned away the lady's maid, Fran, and now stood behind Meg, twisting her hair into a simple chignon. She had stayed with Meg since her return to the house, silent as Fran helped her into a hot bath, talking about nothing important as she was dressed.

Meg knew what her friend was doing. She was giving her a reprieve since they both knew there would not be another for a long time to come.

She appreciated Emma for it, more than she could express.

"I will not do as good a job at this as Fran would," Emma said around the final hairpin pressed between her lips. "But you are beautiful no matter what."

She slid the last pin in and handed Meg a mirror to look at her handiwork. Meg barely did so and turned to smile at Emma. "I'm not sure it matters how I look today."

"Of course it does," Emma said. "*This* is your armor."

Meg stood and walked across her chamber to stand at the window. She looked down at the garden below where a dozen or so of the party guests were gathered, whispering behind fans, conducting animated discussions that could be about only one thing. Her cheeks burned and her chest ached with anxiety.

"Are we going to talk about what happened?" Meg asked.

Emma stepped forward. "Only if you'd like to."

Meg faced her. "We must, mustn't we? After all, what I've done, it will affect you and James. This scandal will be very deep for a long time to come. And you and he are only just married. I'm so sorry to ruin that happiness."

Emma's expression softened. "My dearest, there is nothing anyone on this earth could do to ruin my happiness when it comes to James. As long as he's here in this world and he is at my side, I am complete. So there is no reason to apologize for that." She caught Meg's hands and gently squeezed. "As for the other, yes, you are moving into some muddy waters. I know snippets of what happened from that awful Lord Baxton's gossip. Do you want to tell me the truth?"

"There's so little to tell," Meg whispered. "I was upset about—" She cut herself off, for saying out loud what she had been upset about felt wrong, especially now that so much damage had been done. "I was upset. I went for a walk, Simon followed, then the storm trapped us. Yes, when we were found we were naked, but that was only to allow our clothes to dry out. Nothing...happened."

Emma arched a brow. "The way you say that makes me think a little more than nothing happened."

Meg caught her breath as she looked at her friend. Emma had such a kind expression, a gentle one. And the truth of what had happened last night felt like it was festering in Meg's body. She needed to say it out loud. She needed someone else to understand. "He—he kissed me."

Emma nodded, but didn't look surprised by the admission. "And how was it?"

Meg drew back. "That is what you have to say? No admonishment? No shock?"

"James may be surprised to find out that you have carried feelings for Simon for all these years, but I am not," Emma said with a laughing shake of her head. "I have seen, even just since you and I became good friends a handful of months ago, how close you and Simon are. How much you mean to each other. So, how was the kiss? You have been waiting for it a long time."

Meg shifted, for gossiping like schoolgirls over the kiss seemed untoward. "Perhaps I shouldn't..."

"There is plenty of opportunity for self-recrimination to come," Emma whispered. "Tell me about the kiss. You are allowed to have enjoyed it."

"Graham never kissed me. Not more than on the cheek ever and rarely even that," Meg admitted slowly. "So it was not only my first kiss with Simon, but my first kiss ever. And it was...I have never felt anything like it, Emma. It was tender and passionate, not gentle, but I wanted it so much. I wanted more."

Emma smiled. "And I think we both know that more is what you are about to get. Is it the best of circumstances? No, of course not. But I hope you won't let an odd beginning keep you from a happy ending."

"Like you and James have," Meg said.

Emma looked at the clock on the mantel and gasped. "We are meant to join them momentarily. Come, we'll walk together."

Meg's stomach clenched. "Oh God, I'm not ready. I'm not ready to face Graham, to face James. To face the future."

Emma shook her head. "You think you aren't, but you are stronger than you know. I think you told me that once."

"The difference is that when I told you, it was true."

Her friend touched her cheek gently. "I assure you, it is true when I say it to you, too. Now come."

Emma linked arms with her and they left the chamber, walking down the stairs and through the halls to James's office. Meg's nervousness increased with each step and finally they stopped in front of the closed door. She expected Emma to simply ferry her inside, but she didn't.

Instead her friend turned toward her, a renewed earnestness to her expression. "You were right when you said James and I had an odd start. Our pretended courtship, his vow to marry me to protect me from my father's machinations…all of it could have pushed us far apart as we started our marriage. But I loved him, Meg. And he loved me. Once we admitted that, focused on that…nothing else mattered."

Meg nodded slowly. She understood what Emma was trying to say to her. The difference was that she wasn't entirely certain that Simon loved her. Or that he wanted her, *truly* wanted her, despite the searing kiss in the cottage.

All she knew for certain was that what was about to happen

behind that big, mahogany door was not going to be happy or joyful or celebratory.

Because of what she and Simon had done, it was bound to be much, much worse.

CHAPTER 8

As Meg entered the room, her arm looped through Emma's, Simon staggered to his feet. He, James and Graham had been waiting for them for only a few moments, but it had felt like an eternity. Now he stared at Meg, her cheeks pale, her dark eyes downcast, and everything he'd ever felt for her swelled to the surface.

He loved her, as he always had. And he would marry her. She would be his. But this beginning, it would hang over them. Perhaps it would not be something they could ever overcome. The very idea that it wasn't broke his heart.

He heard Graham clear his throat and turned to see his friend pace away, not looking at either of them. Meg lifted her gaze at last, looking first at the turned back of Graham, then her brother, and finally she swung her eyes on Simon. She caught her breath.

"Oh, Simon," she gasped. "Your nose."

Graham turned sharply at that statement and glared at Simon. Simon forced a half-smile for her and barely kept from a grimace at the pain that shot from the very injury that worried her. "It's fine, Margaret."

She stiffened at the formal use of her name and her gaze slid away as she blushed. Emma frowned in his direction, then guided Meg to James's side and went back to shut and lock the door.

"This room has such a thick barrier," Emma said. "At least those interested parties outside will hear nothing in here."

Simon bent his head. Oh yes, they had already provided far too much fodder for the gossips.

"James," Emma said softly, meeting her husband's eyes.

Simon stared at the gentle encouragement that flitted between them. The way that his friend softened when he was with his wife. Their easy connection was deceptive, of course. Simon knew how hard-fought their love had been.

But now they were happy. He cast his gaze toward Meg and wondered...*hoped*...that perhaps one day that could be his own future.

"Let's just get it over with," Graham said, facing the others at last. "Stop dragging it out." His hard tone and the way he separated himself from the rest of the room made Simon's heart sink.

James cleared his throat. "Very well. Obviously the compromising position Simon and Margaret were caught in has changed the circumstances surrounding her engagement to you, Graham. Perhaps if it had only been you and me who found them as they were, we could have smoothed it over. But with Baxton with us and gleefully spreading his tale...well, that complicates things."

"*Complicates* things," Graham said softly. "That is certainly one way of putting it."

"I think we all know what must happen now," James said, ignoring the angry tone of their friend's voice. "It is obvious that Graham and Meg must end their engagement. And Simon and Meg must marry."

"And quickly," Emma said with a smile of reassurance for Meg.

Graham folded his arms. "I have no quarrel with ending the engagement," he said. "But perhaps you should ask the new couple if they'd like to marry. Arranging a marriage didn't work out so well for you in the past, Abernathe."

James flinched, for none of his closest friends called him by his title. He had always been James to Graham and Simon. Graham was clearly sending a message by saying otherwise.

"You are correct in that I had a part in this," James said. "For which I apologize sincerely. I thought I was doing the right thing. Obviously I wasn't."

Meg shook her head. "You cannot take responsibility for me or for Simon, James."

Her brother shrugged. "Still, Graham has a point. I don't want to repeat the mistakes of the past just to smooth over gossip. Meg, would you like to marry Simon? And Simon, would you marry Meg?"

Simon jolted at the question. The answer was so much more complicated than his friend would ever know. He wasn't even sure he had the words to try to explain how deeply that question touched his heart. A heart he had tried to hide for so long, he wasn't certain how to draw it into the light. Or if he should draw it out at all.

When he was silent, Meg said, "I know that this scandal will likely never fully fade. But a marriage would certainly soften it. I *would* marry Simon, but only if he were not opposed. I will not trap someone into marriage. I'd rather remain a spinster and be sequestered into the country as punishment for what I did."

Simon jolted at the idea of Meg, locked away in some country-side manor, paying for his actions forever. Alone. Her passionate nature stifled. She didn't look at him now as she awaited his response to her statement, but he could see her lower lip trembling ever so slightly and her hands clenched at her sides in fists.

"I would not allow that," he said. "Margaret, I would be… privileged to marry you if you would have me after I've demonstrated such a breach in character and honor."

"So you will each agree," James said and there was no mistaking the relief in his tone. "Then I say we need to make an announcement of the end of one engagement and the beginning of another. To say nothing and simply let the gossip grow would only make it worse. Graham, would you take part in such a thing?"

Graham shook his head slowly. "Help soften the blow, you mean. Act as if I'm fine with what was done?"

Meg took a breath and moved toward her former fiancé. He stiffened as she approached, and Simon tensed as he waited for whatever Meg would do.

"I would *not* ask you to do this," she said. "If you want to call me a whore from the rooftops and leave this house without looking back, I'll take that censure. I've earned it. You were never anything but kind to me and I've repaid you with humiliation and the implication of a worse kind of betrayal. Because of that, I don't deserve anything less than your worst."

Her words, spoken in a wavering but strong tone, seemed to assuage Graham. His expression grew easier and he let out his breath slowly.

"You don't deserve to be destroyed," he said, lifting his gaze to Simon. "I wouldn't do that to you. Yes, Abernathe, I'll do as you say. I'll be part of an announcement. But I would like to leave here as soon as I can. A quiet return to London seems the best answer for everyone. That way you can plan your wedding, as it seems it would be best for these two to rush their engagement."

"Of course," Emma said. "We shall make an announcement this afternoon. Just a quick few words from James as you all stand by."

As Meg stepped away, James stepped forward and held out a hand to Graham. "Thank you."

Graham stared at the offering, then his gaze moved to Meg and to Simon. "A scene won't do any of us any good," he said, not taking James's hand. "Now I'll go up and have my servants prepare my things for immediate departure. Send me word when you will have me join you. I shall do so."

He said nothing else, but left the room in a few long, purposeful strides. He shut the door behind himself, not slamming it, but with a firmness that spoke of endings. Permanent ones.

James slowly lowered the hand that he still held out and bent his head. Emma rushed to his side, taking his arm as he murmured, "He despises me."

"He's hurt," Emma said, smoothing her hand along his back to soothe him. "Right now he is hurt and embarrassed. But time will heal him. And time will let him be open to your friendship again."

"*You* didn't do this to him," Simon said with a shake of his head. "He will forgive you."

What remained unspoken in the room was that Graham would never forgive Simon. And even though they had been more distant in the past few years, the loss of one of his oldest friends cut him. But he deserved to bleed.

"Are we engaged?" Meg asked, her eyes darting to him.

Simon cleared his throat and moved toward her. As much as his heart and soul ached for what he'd done, her question also lit a spark of joy in him. One he tamped down out of decorum.

"Yes," he said softly, reaching for her hand. She let him take it, looking up into his eyes with questions, with fears...but also with desires. The same ones that had flared between them the night before and brought their lives crashing around them.

But now she was his and he could play out those desires to his heart's content.

"Congratulations," James said, clearly trying to brighten his tone. "I should get drinks."

"No," Simon said, turning away from Meg with difficulty. "We will toast the marriage when it comes. I think toasting the engagement would be unseemly in this moment, given the circumstances."

James nodded. "Very well. Then perhaps we should talk details."

Simon released Meg's hand with difficulty and moved to James's desk. Yes, details he could manage. Details were unemotional and technical. Not like the rolling feelings that currently gripped his heart.

Those he would have to get a handle on. They had already caused a great deal of damage.

~

As Meg stood at the top of the garden, overlooking the crowd of guests gathered there, what she wanted more than anything was to slip to Simon's side and take his hand. His presence had always been a comfort to her, but now...

Well, now he was distant, standing next to James, not looking at her as they prepared to make their announcement to the party at large. His face, handsome though swollen from his broken nose, never turned toward her. And the crowd whispered at far too loud a rate about the bruises beneath his eyes and the way Graham stood away from Meg.

"Ladies and gentlemen," James said, his booming voice and no-nonsense tone silencing the party in an instant. "Obviously you have all heard things today." He shot a pointed glance at Lord Baxton, who refused to meet his host's eyes. "And our family *does* have an announcement."

"*I* have an announcement," Graham said, stepping in front of James.

Meg jerked her face toward him. *This* was not what they'd agreed to, and judging from Graham's grim expression, there was no telling what he would now say. She held her breath.

"Seven years ago my closest friend arranged a marriage between myself and his beloved sister," Graham began. "I was lucky to have the chance at a future with such a lady. But recent events have made me realize that she would be better suited to another. So we have mutually ended our engagement."

The crowd let out a collective gasp and the whispers that had been silenced by James's words began again at twice the rate.

Graham turned toward Meg, holding out his hand. She blinked. He was smiling, but it was all a show. She could still see the betrayal, the anger and the deep hurt in his stare. Things he was not expressing out of a goodness and honor that she did not deserve.

She reached out to take his hand. He barely held her hand as he drew her toward Simon and offered it to him.

Simon glanced at the crowd, which was now hanging on this display like it was high theatre. Then he met Graham's eyes and held his gaze there as his friend placed Meg's hand in Simon's.

Graham immediately jerked away and stepped back, behind the families, away from the presentation that clearly was of no pleasure to him. Meg wasn't certain it was of any pleasure to Simon either. He did not look happy as he guided her hand to the crook of his arm and they faced the crowd.

James cleared his throat. "I am happy to announce that Margaret will marry the Duke of Crestwood one week from Saturday in a private ceremony here at Falcon's Landing. There is little else to say in the matter, so I hope you will all simply enjoy the last few days of our gathering and wish the happy couple nothing less than the best. Good day."

He turned and motioned Simon and Meg back toward the house. Graham was already ahead of them, mounting the steps back to the terrace two at a time. Simon guided Meg up, wordless, not looking at her. They entered the parlor with James and Emma at their heels.

Once inside, Graham faced the foursome. "It is done. And I am back to London. My horse is ready and my servants will be taking my things back in the carriage in a few hours."

James stepped forward, his hands outstretched. "Damn it, Graham, please. Don't go like this. Please don't. Not after everything we are to each other, everything we've been through. Don't go like this."

Graham stared at James, and Meg's heart broke. As boys, Graham had been the ultimate protector of James and Simon. She remembered him once coming to blows with a boy three years their elder because he'd said something untoward about Simon, who had been the last to grow into a man's body. She also remembered him rising up in challenge to James and Meg's father when he had been cruel to them during a visit years ago. He'd gotten his ears boxed and never cared.

Now he looked at James and Simon like he didn't even know them.

"I have two options in how I leave," he said softly. "Like this, or in a way that would be far worse. I choose *this* because someday... someday I may not be so angry. But for now, this is all I can do. Goodbye."

His voice cracked as he said the last, then he left the room without so much as a nod. His footfalls led away to the foyer and out where Meg imagined his horse was waiting.

James bent his head and turned back. Simon looked sick. "I'm sorry."

James let out a long sigh. "It doesn't matter now. Here we are. We should make the best of it." He moved toward Meg and smiled at her gently. "I think it might be best if you went upstairs."

"And what about the party?" she asked.

Emma shook her head. "James and I discussed it earlier. We agree that you and Simon should stay away today. Let the worst of the reaction die down while James and I manage it. Tomorrow we will start over. Tomorrow we will plan a small ball to end the party and celebrate the engagement. And James and Simon will take time to arrange the special license and the rest."

Meg nodded, numb when she should have been happy. She would marry Simon in just one week's time. And yet she didn't feel she could celebrate.

With the current mood of the room, this felt more like a time for mourning. All the passion she had felt from Simon in the cottage the night before, all the pleasure and the connection that had pulsed between them and caused this shocking change...it was gone now.

And she worried if she would ever feel such connection from him again.

CHAPTER 9

Meg sat at her dressing table, pulling a brush through her hair over and over, wishing she could just be hypnotized by the strokes and turn her restless mind off. It had been an incredibly trying afternoon.

It would have been bad enough with just the announcement of her new engagement and the drama that surrounded that. But that it was such a public, shocking thing made it impossible to be separated from the consequences. Despite the fact that Meg had been sequestered away, women who called themselves friends kept coming to her door. They were digging for information. Digging for fresh gossip.

They wanted to look at her face and see her pain written across it. Oh, there were a few who were not so cruel about it, but all were intensely curious. All wanted a little kernel of the story they could repeat later.

She was exhausted and only wanted to go to her bed and forget this day. She sighed and stood up, shrugging from her dressing gown and moving toward her bed. Fran had turned it down before she left half an hour before, and as Meg smoothed her hand over the cool, clean sheets she let out a sigh. Yes, things always looked better after a good night's sleep.

They had to.

She was about to climb into those sheets and blow out her candle when there was a light knock at her chamber door. She turned to face it, lips pinched. She had said goodnight to James hours ago, Emma had come to check on her more recently, Fran should be happily in her own bed.

Which meant it was probably more tourists to her emotions on the other side of the door. To come here at midnight certainly took guts.

"Ignore it," she murmured to herself as she turned back to the bed once more.

But the knock came again, this time with more force and urgency. She squeezed her eyes shut, frustration about this entire situation finally rising up in her. She stormed to the door and tore it open as she snapped, "There is nothing to discuss!"

But she didn't find herself looking at some grasping lady seeking gossip or even a friend trying to wrap her head around what Meg had done. She found herself staring at a broad chest and lifted her gaze to see that Simon stood in the hall. In the dark. His jacket was off, his shoes were off, his cravat was undone and his hair was mussed, like he'd been running a hand through it.

"S-Simon," she stammered.

He did not smile, but cocked his head. "If you don't want to see me—"

"No," she interrupted, and watched his shoulders slump. She caught his hand. "No, I simply thought you were someone else. *Yes,* I want to see you. I'm sorry. Just—just come in."

She stepped back, keenly aware for the first time that she was clad only in a thin nightrail, her shoulders all but bare but for a pair of inch-wide straps. She blushed, though it was silly. The previous night she had only been clad in a blanket.

Still, she grabbed for her robe and tied it around her waist as Simon entered the room and shut the door behind him.

"Who did you think I was?" he asked.

She shrugged, forcing herself to face him and behave as though all this was perfectly normal. That he was supposed to be in her bedroom in the middle of the night, that he was supposed to be her fiancé. That nothing had changed since yesterday morning, even though everything in her world was different.

She had no other idea how to act but that.

"I have been plagued by interested parties all afternoon," she admitted.

His jaw tightened. "Interested parties? What does that mean?"

"Friends who want to ask me about my new engagement. Congratulate me privately," she said, then shook her head. "They want to spy and get a glimpse of me. You know how these scandals go."

He scowled. "And James and Emma are not preventing this?"

"They aren't my keepers," she said. "Even if they were, what can they do? Stand guard at my door all day?"

"Yes, if they must," he huffed out. "I'll do it myself if they won't."

His protectiveness touched her heart in a way that felt very dangerous considering their current circumstance, but she smiled regardless. "Don't you think that would only make talk worse? No, if I let them in and talk to them as if this new engagement is perfectly normal, then perhaps they'll get bored of the topic sooner and we'll regain some semblance of normalcy."

Simon bent his head and silence filled the room. She stared at him, as he wasn't looking at her. One thing she'd always loved about this man was the light that seemed to surround him. He always had a half-grin, a chuckle. He could lighten even the darkest of situations. He was the first person who made her laugh after her father died.

Tonight, though, that light was gone. The man before her was serious and grim. Pained. She understood why, but she hated that this is where they'd come to after so many years of easy friendship and connection.

She didn't want to lose that. Slowly, she moved to him and extended her hand. They both watched as she took his, intertwining their fingers the way they'd previously only been allowed to do while dancing. His breath caught and he turned toward her slightly.

"Why did you come here tonight?" she whispered. "To my chamber, after everyone else has gone to bed?"

He swallowed, his throat working and he edged closer, cutting off the small distance that remained between them. Now they were almost touching, their bodies a hair's breadth apart.

"You know what I wanted last night," he whispered.

The hand he wasn't holding began to shake and she clenched it into a fist. "I-I think so," she answered. "The same thing I-I wanted."

He squeezed his eyes shut, a low groan coming from deep within his chest. The heat in the room changed, rising as he released her hand and instead slid his fingers around her waist. He tugged her, drawing her fully against him.

"Last night...I couldn't. Because you weren't mine," he continued.

She nodded, understanding that. Understanding how desperately he'd been trying to honor his friend, his claim. "But I'm yours now," she murmured.

He glided his hands through her hair, cupping the back of her head and tilting her face toward his. "I want to make you mine," he said. "Will you let me make you mine?"

She didn't answer, but lifted up and pressed her lips to his. There was a shudder of relief that passed between them, an echo of what she'd felt when he kissed her last night. Only this time there was no guilt to go along with it. There was nothing but the passion that had been long denied, but always there, waiting to be unleashed. His mouth opened and he traced her lips with his tongue. She welcomed him in as she lifted her arms around his neck and pressed herself against him.

They stood that way, kissing, for what felt like an eternity. She memorized every hollow and curve of his mouth, she swam in his taste and the feel of him worshipping her lips. It was heaven.

Finally he pulled back, resting his forehead against hers as his ragged breath moved in and out. "I have wanted to do that for so damn long, Meg."

She smiled as she smoothed her fingers against his shoulders, feeling the muscles there bunch, feeling his own hands tighten at her waist. "I've been waiting too."

He reached down and slid his finger into the knot in her robe's sash. Gently he unwrapped the scrap of silk and then met her stare as he glided his hands up her arms, catching the edge and drawing it down. The room was warm from the fire, but she shivered as he tossed her robe aside.

He stepped back and looked at her from head to toe, his pupils dilating and his fingers clenching. Then he reached up and unbuttoned his own shirt, stripping it open in a few swift actions and throwing it to the floor.

She caught her breath. Last night she'd seen him like this, of course, but she'd stolen those glances. Tonight she had no reason to do so, and she stared long and hard as she moved forward and reached out to place a palm flat against his chest. The solid muscle that greeted her was warm and she felt his heart beat beneath his skin.

Simon caught his breath, but he didn't back away as she spread her fingers across his flesh, exploring every bump and hollow. She forced her gaze up to his face, blushing as their eyes met. He smiled, the first time she'd seen him smile since they'd been caught in the rain together. Then he slid his fingers beneath her nightrail strap and glided one side down.

She gasped as the warm air in the room touched her bare breast, and turned her face so she wouldn't see him looking at her. She heard his sharp intake of breath. When his fingers brushed against her hard nipple, she jerked her attention back to him.

He was staring intently as he stroked his hand back and forth across her. It was like nothing she'd ever felt before, like she was alive in a way she hadn't realized was possible. Tingles of pleasure and awareness shot out from her breast, down into her stomach, lower between her legs, and she could no longer draw a full breath.

He stroked a thumb over her and she grabbed for his forearms, digging her fingers into him as she gasped out surprise at the intensity of the sensations.

His smile widened a little and he reached out to draw down the other strap of her nightrail. He bared her from the waist up and then tugged, bringing the flimsy fabric down over her hips to pool around her feet.

She was naked. Naked with Simon. But not like last night, when there had been blankets and emotions and lies between them. Tonight she was *truly* naked with this man. And he was touching her. Her entire body quaked and she knew her eyes were wide and her gaze uncertain. What she wanted she could not name, what he was doing she didn't fully understand and what would happen next she feared.

Despite it all she wanted more. More touching. More of him. More of what they'd started the night before. More of what was now theirs to take. She wanted everything and she trusted that what he was about to give would be magical.

He covered her other breast, cupping both now in his warm hands. She tilted her head back, reveling in the intensity of his touch, in the way her body arched into him, demanding what she was too shy to ask for with words.

Then she felt the steamy warmth of his breath near her nipple. She opened her eyes and watched as he leaned in and gently circled the nub with the tip of his tongue.

"Simon," she gasped, her hands coming up into his hair. She

tugged him closer, she pushed him away, she nearly toppled over as she tried to process everything she was feeling.

He straightened and looked down into her eyes. "Do you want this?"

"I'm not sure I even know what *this* is," she admitted. "Engaged or not, my mother wasn't exactly explaining anything to me. And I hadn't asked Emma yet."

He pursed his lips. "I'll take you, Meg. I'll put my body into yours."

She nodded. "That part I know. Understanding is different, but I know."

He reached out and caught her hand, pressing it to the front of his trousers where she felt the hard line of his cock. She'd seen just a momentary glimpse of it last night. Big was what she remembered.

Intimidating.

"Will it hurt?" she asked, stroking her fingers up and down that fascinating length through the fabric.

He grunted out a sound that she wasn't sure was pleasure or pain. "At first. Yes."

She cupped him and he jolted. "But not always?"

"No," he said, his voice strangled.

"Am I hurting you?" she asked softly.

"No," he said, his tone stronger. He pushed her hands away and unfastened his trousers. He dropped them and kicked them away and now he stood before her, as naked as she was.

She caught her breath. Stolen glimpses in the dark didn't do him justice. His body was…amazing. Hard where she was soft, broad where she was narrow, and the cock…that cock that he claimed he would fit into her. It was as tempting as it was terrifying.

She reached for him once more and took him in hand. This time there were no barriers between them and she sucked in a gasp of surprise at how hard he was. But the skin was so soft. She smoothed her fingers over the bulging head and down the long, thick shaft.

He pushed into her as she did so and let out a quiet curse. She looked up, fascinated by how enraptured he was. His breath was short, his eyes glazed, his body all tension and coiled strength. He could take over any time he wanted, she sensed that, but he didn't. He just let her stroke him, over and over.

"Keep that up and I'm going to spend," he managed to choke out.

She stopped moving her hand. "What does that mean?"

"That you'll give me so much pleasure I'll lose control and spend my seed before I even have a chance to touch you," he explained, catching her wrist and setting her hand away from him. "And I've waited so long for this, Meg, I have no intention of ending it that way."

He pushed her back toward her bed, guiding her until her legs hit the side of the mattress. Then he swept her up and deposited her on her pillows and climbed up beside her, caging her in with his arms. Although she wasn't certain what to do, her body seemed to move of its own accord, lifting into him as she wound her arms around his neck and drew him in for another of those deep, earth-shattering kisses.

He gave gently, almost reverently, stroking her with his tongue, kissing her until she relaxed into the pillows. Then his mouth drew lower, his lips tasting the angle of her jaw, the curve of her neck, the expanse of her chest and back to her exquisitely sensitive breasts.

She slid her hands into his hair again, able to fully surrender now that she was no longer trying to remain upright as he teased and tasted her. He sucked one nipple, then the other. He nibbled her sensitive flesh with just the edge of his teeth, he sucked until she bit back a cry, he stroked with his tongue until she trembled.

She was needy and on fire, she was shaking and ready to beg. But he pulled his mouth away and traced it lower. Over her ribcage, past her stomach, across her hip, and then he placed one hand on each of her thighs and opened her.

She jolted up to her elbows, staring as he settled between her legs, his face just inches from the most private place in her body. And if that shocked her mind, her sex was another story. Already it was wet, tingling, and having him so near made her hips rise when she didn't recall wanting them to do so.

He smiled and looked up at her. "You can trust me," he whispered.

She tensed at those words. He was saying he would take care of her. That because of his experience, he could make this night one of pleasure for her. The idea was wonderful, indeed, but it made her think of her brother's words earlier in the day.

Of all the other women Simon had done this to. Of all of those he had loved and forgotten in his wake.

But before her worries could overcome her and steal the pleasure of this moment, he dropped his mouth to her and licked her gently. Her mind emptied of everything she thought, everything she might have said. She found herself clutching at the coverlet as he spread her open wide and licked her again.

It was spectacular. Intimate and wicked, focused and far more pleasurable than when he'd done the same to her nipples. She lifted her hips into him, grinding them against him with some kind of ancient, wanton knowledge. The act made the pleasure more focused and he worked his tongue faster over her, gliding his mouth across her center, rolling his tongue around the nub of nerves at the top. She turned her face into her arm, trying to hold back unstoppable gasps and cries as he brought her to the brink of madness with his skilled tongue.

And just when she thought the pleasure couldn't be better, just when she thought she'd reached the pinnacle, her sex began to quake. Tremors of pleasure washed over her and she jolted her hips wildly as he ran his tongue over her again and again and again.

Only when she'd stopped shaking did he lift his head from between her legs, crawling back up to cover her, resting his hands on either side of her head as he stared down into her face.

"I'm ready," she whispered when he was silent for so long she feared he was contemplating running. "I want this."

He shut his eyes, and for a moment there was a flash of pain on his face. A flash of regret that grabbed her heart and squeezed. But then he opened his eyes again and whispered, "I'll give you everything you want then, Meg. Everything."

CHAPTER 10

S imon stared down at Meg, still flushed from her orgasm, her eyes glazed with want but also worry. How many nights had he dreamed of doing just this? How many times had he pleasured himself while picturing her writhing beneath him, surrendering herself to him?

And now he was here. He had already worshipped her body, he had already coaxed out her pleasure. All that was left was this final claiming. This last thing that would make her his.

But all he could think about was the pain he would cause. The physical pain of taking her had begun to represent all the other pain he would bring to her life from this day forward. The whispers today had been harsh. They had been cruel, even.

And there would be more to come. Because of him.

"Simon?" she whispered, lifting up slightly and reaching out to touch his cheek.

He let out a shuddering sigh and leaned into her gentle fingers. "I don't want to hurt you," he admitted. "But there is no avoiding it."

She tilted her head and examined him, and he thought she understood he wasn't just talking about this night, this moment.

"You told me it wouldn't always hurt—did you lie?" she whispered.

He shook his head. "No. No, after the first time it should never hurt again, if I am doing my job right."

She smiled. "Then the pain leads to something better."

He winced. "Meg—"

She reached between them and gently touched his cock, placing him at her entrance. "I want this, Simon. All of it. If the pain is part of it, then I want that too. Because all the feelings, the good and the bad, make it real. Make it true. Please."

It was the please that hit him in the gut. She said it so softly, so gently, not as a plea on her behalf, but on his. And he had never been able to deny her. Not since the first moment he saw her. Certainly not since the moment he recognized she was not just a woman, but the woman for him.

And for better or for worse, for good or for bad, for whatever he had done to bring them here...now they *were* here. And while he wasn't certain he would ever be worthy of loving her, if he was even capable of giving her what she needed, when it came to pleasure... there he was an expert.

He drew in a long breath, then met her eyes once more. As he focused on the deep brown depths, he pushed her legs just a little wider with his knee. He kept her stare even as he began to breach her.

And it was heaven. From the moment he slid inside, her body gripped him, a tight, wet glove that welcomed him home like he belonged there. He felt the resistance of her unused channel, knew when the pain hit by the way she caught her breath.

He stopped even though it took a lion's share of control to do so, and stroked her cheek with his hand. "Relax," he murmured.

She nodded. "It's only a little pain," she reassured him. "It's so strange to have another person inside of me."

He smiled and leaned in, pressing his mouth to hers. She opened to him immediately, his tongue stroking hers, just as he would stroke her with his body in a moment. When he felt her relax beneath him, her inner muscles flex and flutter, he pushed forward again.

She gasped into his mouth, but her arms didn't unwind from his neck, her kiss didn't stop and her body accepted him inch by inch until he was fully seated inside of her.

It was the most powerful thing he had ever experienced. Oh, he'd fucked plenty of women before, he'd found a great deal of pleasure in that act. But it was fleeting. This was something different. This was a woman he loved. A woman he'd been certain he would lose.

And now he was inside of her, her body flexing around him, her breath against his neck as she clung to him. He'd never felt such pleasure before and he hadn't even started moving.

He flexed his hips gently, testing her response, and she let out a soft sound. "Does it hurt?" he asked.

She shook her head. "No," she groaned. "Not hurt."

He smiled at the tension in her voice, brought about by pleasure, and rolled his hips again. "Does it feel good?"

"Oh God," she grunted, her fingernails digging slightly into his back. "Yes."

He crushed his mouth down on hers and began to take her in long, steady strokes. She lifted to meet him, her innocence not as strong as her natural drive to find pleasure and to take his. And took his, she did. His cock had never felt so hard or so sensitive as he drove through her wet folds and ground against her already sensitive clitoris.

She was moaning now, her cries just a little too loud for the house full of people. He covered her mouth with his, letting her gasp and groan into him as he took her over and over again. His balls tightened, he knew he was going to spend, but he wanted her to come again. He wanted to mark her with pleasure before he marked her with his seed.

And then she cried out his name and her body began to flutter, massaging him with her inner muscles as orgasm hit her again. She stared up at him, eyes wide with both surprise and pleasure, and he could hold back no more. He thrust a few more times as she milked him and then allowed himself to find release as he came inside of her.

He collapsed down over her, feeling the softness of her body as her arms came around and held him. Her fingers smoothed along his spine as she pressed warm, sweet kisses against his neck and his shoulders. Simon let out a deep sigh. He had been waiting for this all his life, it seemed. And here he was. And she was his.

He had stolen her, of course.

That thought made his eyes come open and he rolled away from her onto his back, separating their bodies as the tightness around his chest returned in an instant.

Meg moved to her side and settled her head on his shoulder as she rested a hand on his chest. "I'm so glad you came here tonight," she murmured, tracing a light pattern on his skin with the tips of her fingernails. "To be honest, I-I thought you might be angry with me."

He looked down at her. "Angry?" he repeated. "Why?"

"Because you're being forced to marry me," she said with a sigh. "After you didn't do anything wrong."

He sat up slightly and it forced her to move. "Didn't do anything wrong?" he repeated. "Can you be serious?"

She swallowed as she sat up, as well. "I only meant—"

"I followed you when I should have gotten your brother or your fiancé to do so," he said. "I did it because I wanted you. And yes, being trapped in the cottage was not my fault specifically, but I kissed you, Meg. Because I wanted you. I have coveted you for years. Coveted what my friend had, and now I've taken it."

Her lips parted and there was a flash of anger in her eyes. "Simon, I'm not a prize that can be passed from man to man. You didn't steal a horse or a ring from Graham. You can't *steal* a person."

He turned his head. "Perhaps not, but here we are, aren't we?"

She pushed from the bed and walked away, grabbing for her

discarded robe and flinging it around her shoulders. As she tied it, he tried to push away his disappointment that she would want to cover herself.

She stared at him. "If you hate yourself, hate *me*, so much for what you've done, then why come here? Why make love to me? Why want me to have pleasure?"

He frowned as he got up. He saw her gaze flit to his cock and felt life begin to flow back into it. With a grunt of self-loathing, he turned away and grabbed his trousers, pulling them on before he said, "I don't hate you. But I came here tonight because...because..."

He stopped. He'd been trying very hard not to analyze why he came to her door. He'd been thinking about her all day. All night. And somehow he'd just arrived there, knowing what he would do. Knowing what he wanted and would take because there was no longer someone standing in his way.

But *why*? That was something much darker.

"Why?" she repeated.

He gritted his teeth. "So that no one else could take you away. So that nothing could stop what is going to happen."

She was silent, her expression stunned by the confession he hadn't wanted to make to himself, let alone to her. The confession that he was little better than a thief who had come last night...and tonight.

"I have altered both our worlds, Meg," he said softly. "And in the process I have destroyed a great many people I care for. All because I wanted you and was willing to do anything to have you. *That* is why I hate myself. That is why I don't deserve happiness. Not while I have made so many others suffer for my selfishness."

He moved toward the door.

"You're leaving?" she asked.

He froze, hand at the door, and sighed. "We are not married yet, Meg. I-I don't belong here." With great difficulty, he left the room, left her. And as he shut the door and leaned on it in the hallway, he whispered, "I never did."

~

M eg stifled a yawn and forced a smile as Emma poured her a cup of tea. "Thank you."

"Unless you want something stronger," Emma said, sitting down beside her and resting a hand gently on her stomach. Meg's smile grew more real as she did, for she knew that Emma's pregnancy was a great joy to her brother and his wife.

At least there was that, though she couldn't imagine all this strain was good for Emma or the child.

"I'm fine. You should worry about you," Meg said, reaching out to cover her hand and smiling as she felt Emma's tiny belly beneath. No one except those who had been told would know yet.

"I'm not worried about me, I'm wonderful," Emma reassured her. "But since your mother has not yet joined us for the planning for this final ball, I wonder if there's anything you'd like to discuss with me. Is there any way I can help?"

Meg got up and paced away. She couldn't help but think of the previous night. Of Simon's body against hers, inside of hers, of all the pleasure she had experienced.

Just before he walked out the door.

She sent a side glance at Emma and found her friend waiting, quiet but expectant. She opened her mouth, but couldn't find the words.

She blushed. "Will I be allowed to join the others tonight?"

Emma got to her feet with a gasp. "Dearest, you aren't imprisoned. Great Lord, James and I only thought you might need a break from prying eyes and loud whispers. I know you haven't had much of one with all the visitors to your door—"

Meg jolted at that statement and the memories of Simon at her door. But Emma was unaware and continued talking.

"—but of course you will join the group for supper tonight. And we'll all lift our chins and have a brave face. Isn't that what you told me not that long ago when I was confronting a humiliating experience?"

Meg smiled. "Your father trying to arrange a terrible marriage for you and James's interference aren't exactly the same things as what Simon and I have done." She sighed. "Perhaps Simon is right that we deserve punishment. I've hurt our family, after all."

Emma shook her head. "Neither of you deserves punishment. And this final ball is to prove that our family supports the union, Meg. Which we do. James and I *fully* support you."

Meg blinked back the tears that suddenly stung her eyes. Of course James and Emma supported her. James had always been willing to do anything to protect her, including the engagement to Graham that had started this mess all those years ago. And Emma was patently incapable of doing anything but be sympathetic and loving. It didn't change that both of them were being swept up in the wake of this scandal, even if Emma refused to acknowledge that fact.

Before Meg could say more, though, her mother strolled into the room. Meg turned toward her with a frown. The dowager looked fine to any casual observer, but Meg was not that. There were shadows beneath her mother's eyes and a glazed look to her that meant one thing: she was hungover. A usual occurrence.

Emma sent Meg a supportive look, for she knew just as well as Meg the damage the dowager could do, and moved to the door to welcome her.

"There you are," Emma said with a broad smile. "Just in time, for we were only beginning to talk about the final ball of the party. Meg's engagement ball."

The dowager sent Meg a brief look, and Meg shifted beneath her regard. Her mother was often hard to read, thanks to her emotions being blunted by alcohol. Today, though, she saw worry in the dowager's eyes. Perhaps even judgment.

And if she had earned the judgment of a woman who often had

to be snuck out of parties so she didn't make a scene, how far Meg had fallen, indeed.

"I think the most important thing is that we act like this is the first ball we've ever held in honor of Meg's engagement," the dowager said, moving to pour herself tea and drinking deeply before she continued, "If anyone is so uncouth as to mention the Duke of Northridge, we move on as if his name was never mentioned."

Meg frowned. "Graham is...*was*...such a good friend to both James and Simon. And we were engaged for so long, Mother. I don't know that pretending he doesn't exist will help."

Her mother arched a brow. "The young man left here in order to protect you all in some way, did he not?"

Meg's forehead wrinkled as she thought of Graham's hasty and angry departure. At the time, she wasn't certain he was thinking of her or Simon in any kind of protective way. But then again, if he'd stayed it only would have caused larger rumblings. More to stare at and analyze.

And the one thing Graham had always been was protective. Of James, of Simon...even of her.

"If part of his leaving was to protect Simon and me, then we owe him a great deal," she said softly.

"And one day I'm certain you will have a chance to make all this up to him," the dowager said with a dismissive wave of her hand. "But for now, I say we make this a glittering ball, a powerful display of our family unity and celebration of this union."

Emma ran a hand across her chin, as if she were pondering the suggestion. "I thought small and demure, but you are likely right. A larger display will show our support and perhaps silence those who would find fault in this match."

"A good party will silence *anyone* if done properly," the dowager said.

Emma nodded. "I agree. But since this party is tomorrow night, that means I must rush off to speak to the servants now and adjust our plans. Will you two be…" She darted her gaze to Meg. "Will you be all right?"

"Of course," the dowager said. "Meg and I have lived together for years, of course we can be alone together."

Meg nodded to allow Emma to leave. She did so, but Meg could see she was uncertain. Truth be told, so was she as she turned toward her mother.

"Now that Emma is gone, do you have anything to say to me, Mother?"

The dowager flinched ever so slightly at the question, but she didn't back away. "You think I was holding back my judgments of you until Emma left?"

Meg shrugged. "I suppose if you had judgments, Emma's presence wouldn't have prevented you from stating them. I only thought you might want to scold me since you didn't get the chance to do so yesterday when this mess began."

"Because I was drunk," her mother said.

Meg's mouth dropped open in shock. The dowager had never acknowledged that she drank, not in all the years Meg had been tasked with watching her, protecting her, keeping her from public view when she was at her worst.

"I-I—"

Her mother shook her head. "Don't you ever wonder *why* I escape in a bottle, Margaret?"

Meg turned her face slightly. "I know why. You were very unhappy with Father."

"Do you? Do you truly understand? Perhaps you do, considering this broken engagement and compromising position you found yourself in." The dowager let out a pained sigh. "Your father had a family before ours. The family he truly wanted. When they were killed in that accident, he didn't want to marry again or have new children."

Meg pursed her lips. Although this was not a conversation she had ever had with her mother, over the years she had discussed it with James…with Simon…and she'd *tried* to understand her father. Tried to feel for him and the grief he must have endured when he lost the family he'd chosen.

But that was hard when his cruelty toward her and her brother was so abject.

"He had his duty, though, didn't he?" she said softly.

The dowager nodded. "Indeed, he did. And that duty was important to him. Our marriage was also arranged. My father's fortune was good and his title was respected. It was a good match, at least on paper. The reality, as you know, was far different."

"He hated us all," Meg murmured. "I don't think he spoke to me at all from the time I was seven or eight until the day he died. I was unimportant, not a boy, not a spare."

Her mother shuddered. "He hardly spoke to me, either. He grunted over me, trying to produce a spare out of terror that his eldest son would die, but after you were born, we never conceived again. He hated me for it. He hated you for being a girl. He hated James for not being his late son."

"Did you ever love him?" Meg asked softly, emboldened by this mother who was so open about the past.

She seemed to ponder the answer for a long moment.

"No," she said at last. "In fact, I was…I was in love with someone else when the marriage was thrust upon me. I lost him and the future I had pictured. So I suppose there was enough resentment to go around between your father and me. The point is, Margaret, that marrying someone I did not love or even like only created misery for us all. It made me…*this*. It ultimately led me to fail you and James."

Meg lifted a hand to her lips, for this additional acknowledgment of the dowager's shortcomings was unexpected. "Mama," she whispered, reverting to a less formal address than she usually used.

The dowager lifted her chin. "I know what I am, Margaret. And despite my flaws, I do…care for you. I don't want to see you become what I am. I know you love your brother, I know he believes he's doing what is right for you, but do not let anyone force you into what you don't want."

Meg bent her head. "The first engagement, to Graham...I didn't want it. I was too young to argue and then the situation was so far gone I didn't think I could. Perhaps in that scenario, I would have ended up...unhappy. But with Simon, it is different. I do want to marry him, Mother."

Her mother smiled. It was such a rare expression, and for a moment Meg caught her breath, for she saw her brother in her mother's face. She saw herself. She saw whatever could have been for a young woman before she was forced into a loveless, desperately unhappy marriage.

"Then don't let go," the dowager said. She cleared her throat and her usual sour expression returned. "My head is throbbing now. I think I shall go find something a bit stronger than tea. Good afternoon, Margaret."

Her mother left and Meg sank hard into the closest chair to ponder their unexpected conversation. This moment of clarity was not one that would last, she would wager. There was too much pain for her mother to overcome without the help of alcohol. But this was the first time she'd connected with her mother in years— decades, even. And that she could, even in this dark moment, gave her hope.

A hope she decided to cling to with both hands as she faced the uncertain future with a man she no longer understood.

CHAPTER 11

Simon stood in the billiard room, watching as the Duke of Roseford, the Earl of Idlewood and James played a round. By entering the room late, he'd excluded himself from participating, but he was just as happy. Tonight he was in no mood for games.

He was in no mood for a ball, either, but that was what was about to start in less than an hour. Worse, it was his engagement ball and the final event at the country party before the others made their way back to London. The final event before he married Meg and made her his.

His in name. In body, he had already claimed her. Since then, he had avoided her, trying to rein in his lust and his feelings and all the things that had led them to this place. If he didn't, he feared he'd be swept up in her and not recall what he'd done to get her.

"Will the Duchess of Crestwood be joining the party for the wedding?" Robert asked after he'd taken a shot and passed his cue to Christopher.

Simon flinched, dragged back into the conversation by both the question and the topic. It was yet another unhappy one, for his relationship with his mother had long been strained, to say the least.

"She is my only family, so I've asked her to come," he said. "I sent word two days ago. The message should have reached her today, and if she departed tomorrow to join us, that would have her arrive here at Falcon's Landing by Tuesday evening at the latest."

"Your *only* family," Kit said softly. "That wasn't always the case, was it? I mean, weren't *we* supposed to be like brothers?"

James straightened and shot their friend a look. "Idlewood," he said, a gentle warning.

But Christopher didn't seem deterred. He faced Simon, crossing his arms across his chest. "We talked about this the night Meg and Northfield announced the date of their wedding. Didn't we?"

Robert and James swung their attention to Simon and both looked confused at the reference. Simon gritted his teeth. "You asked me about my...my situation when it came to Meg and Graham, yes."

"And in that moment you told me you recognized it was helpless, hopeless, because to act on those thoughts or feelings was to betray a friend. But here we are, aren't we?"

"Enough," James said, setting his cue aside and physically stepping between the two men. "This is not helpful, Idlewood. Simon is obviously punishing himself enough for his part in this situation."

"As I should," Simon said, turning away from his friends. "I *deserve* Idlewood's censure, as I do all of yours. Our friendship, our club, was about brotherhood and support, honor and fealty. That meant the world to me, but I still broke those vows, I don't claim I did anything else. Because of that, I don't deserve *anything* but the contempt of Idlewood and the hatred Graham feels for me. I don't turn away from it or make any excuse where I can free myself from it. I'll carry what I did for the rest of my life."

As Simon looked back at the men, Kit's expression gentled slightly, but he remained with his arms folded. Simon could well imagine that with Graham's return to London, once the story of what had happened here with Meg spread far and wide, the others in their club would very likely take sides. They might talk to him still, they might be gentlemanly about it, but clearly he would lose friends over this.

He deserved nothing less.

James stepped forward. "The ball will begin in about ten minutes. Perhaps we should join the others, yes?"

Robert cleared his throat, his gaze moving to Simon. "Should we toast the engagement before we do?"

Simon stiffened at that question. Then he shook his head. "No," he said softly, and left the room without another word.

Already guests were entering the ballroom at the end of the long hallway and he heard arrivals of other partygoers from the foyer. He drew in a long breath, set his shoulders back and strode down to join the party.

Meg's cheeks hurt from the false smile that had been plastered onto her face for the past half an hour. A brave face, Emma called it, and her friend occasionally reached out to squeeze her hand and offer support as they stood together at the edge of the dancefloor with James at Emma's side.

"So far I would call tonight a success," James said, though Meg heard the faint tension in his tone.

She felt the same tension in herself. A success, it seemed, was to be measured in the fact that there had been no scandal and people were still speaking to her. A low bar to calculate by, indeed. Especially when she looked across the room and saw her fiancé standing alone.

He would not look at her.

Simon's avoidance, which had begun the day after they made love, stung more than a lash could have. She would have preferred a physical blow at this point. At least that kind of wound presented a chance at recovery if it was treated. But this dragged-out distance that now seemed to loom up between her and Simon...

That was something else entirely. And the longer it went on, the more it permanently scarred her, scarred *them*.

Emma's foot tapped beneath the hem of her gown, and Meg sent her a side glance. Once a wallflower, Emma had been reluctant to dance at first. But a few months of marriage to James and Meg knew the new duchess had grown very fond of spinning around in a quadrille or tucking herself into James's arms for a waltz. Soon enough her growing belly would prevent her from doing either.

"You two should dance," Meg said, waving them toward the floor. "You haven't since the party began, and if we are pretending all this is normal and right, then you must behave as you would at any ball. With you two that means dancing so close you scandalize the Upper Ten Thousand."

Emma blushed, but for the first time tonight, James grinned. "I *do* like to scandalize the Upper Ten Thousand when I can."

Emma swatted him on the arm gently. "James!"

He caught her hand and drew her closer. "Come, Emma, let's turn all their eyes on us, shall we?"

He smiled at Meg, then guided his wife away. Meg could see him murmuring to Emma, close to her ear, and Emma eyes went wide in response. True to his word, he held her far too close as the strains of the waltz began.

Meg sighed at the love they so easily displayed. They had overcome so much to have their moment, their future. She didn't begrudge them that, but she was also more starkly aware of her own dire situation when she observed it.

"Good evening, Lady Margaret."

Meg stiffened and turned toward the female voice that had said her name. Her frown deepened as she realized the person who had joined her was Sarah Carlton. She was the same girl who had danced with Simon earlier in the party, the girl Meg had been jealous of when she had no right. Judging from the sour look on her new companion's face, it seemed the jealousy now cut both ways.

"Miss Carlton, isn't it?" she asked, trying to strike a friendly, breezy tone.

The young woman nodded once and stepped up next to her, observing those on the dancefloor for a moment.

"Are you enjoying yourself?" Meg asked, struggling to behave as she would normally.

Miss Carlton shrugged. "I *was*."

"Oh," Meg said, praying this wasn't about to become a conversation about her. "Is there something I can do for you, since our hosts are currently dancing?"

Miss Carlton turned on her, eyes narrowing. Meg's chest tightened at the look, for it was clear this woman's ire was directed at her. And there could be but one subject.

The one she was trying hard to avoid.

"You had a fiancé," Miss Carlton hissed, thankfully not too loudly. "A perfectly good fiancé who was a duke. I think an even richer duke than Crestwood, if my mother is to be believed."

Meg clenched her fists at her sides. "You and I do not know one another well enough to be having this incredibly impertinent conversation."

"I don't care if it's impertinent," Miss Carlton said with a toss of her blonde hair. "Great God, is any man safe? Will you bore of the Duke of Crestwood soon enough and move on to another? Will you suck up all the eligible men in the countryside and leave none for anyone else?"

"You have *no* idea what you are talking about," Meg snapped, her patience wearing thin. "Crestwood and I have been friends a very long time and—"

"*Friends*, my lady? Only *friends*?" the other woman said, dark and cruel implication dripping from the words.

Miss Carlton blinked, and Meg could see frustrated and desperate tears in her eyes. She didn't know the woman well, but she remembered Miss Carlton was in a rather bad financial state. If she'd convinced herself that Simon had liked her when they danced,

Meg could understand why she would feel something had been taken from her. Something Meg herself didn't need.

And Meg wanted to feel compassion for the woman. But right now all she felt was a desire to escape her censure and her anger.

"You are overwrought," Meg said firmly. "And perhaps you've had too much punch."

"I am not overwrought," the other woman muttered. "I just don't like to see someone grab for everything in the world because she thinks she can just take, take, take. My only consolation is that this scandal is so desperate that you may never recover. And when they whisper about you, I shall be the first one to tell them what *I* observed with my own two eyes."

"That is enough."

Both women turned and Meg's cheeks flamed bright. The Earl of Idlewood was now standing just at her side, glaring down at Miss Carlton. He was an old friend of James, Simon and Graham, one of their club of dukes. In fact, he was the only one who hadn't yet inherited his ultimate title.

Meg knew him, of course, for he had visited her brother many times over the years. They had always been cordial. But since the incident with Graham, she had sometimes felt his eyes on her… judging. Idlewood was loyal, and she sensed he condemned her on her lack of that quality.

"Lord Idlewood," Miss Carlton said, her gaze darting away. "I did not see you there."

"I would wager not, or you would not have said such wretched things," Idlewood said softly. "Walk away now and go back to your mother. I'd also suggest you start planning on how you're to tell her."

"Tell her?" Miss Carlton squeaked out.

Idlewood arched a brow. "When the Duke of Abernathe finds out you were attacking his sister, your invitations to many events are going to disappear. I assume you'll need to tell your mother why. Now run along."

Miss Carlton's lips pressed together tightly and then she turned and walked across the room. Meg let out the breath she hadn't even known she was holding and glanced up at Idlewood.

"Thank you," she said. "For coming to my aid."

He looked down at her, and there was still a dismissive air to him as he sniffed, "I could not allow the sister of one of my closest friends to be spoken to in that manner."

Meg swallowed. "Even if you agree with the words being said?"

Idlewood's jaw went tense and he stared off into the crowd. She realized he was looking at Simon, and there was regret on his face.

"I, unlike Miss Carlton, recognize the situation is far more complicated than a mere compromising position." He shook his head slowly. "Are you going to tell Abernathe what she said to you? If you won't, I will."

Meg's lips parted. "I appreciate your desire to stand up for me, despite your misgivings about my character. But Miss Carlton is already in a precarious position. You were right when you said that James would be angry if he heard she talked to me like that. I don't want to be responsible for her losing any chances in Society."

Idlewood's brow wrinkled. "You'd let it pass?"

She nodded. "I would. I do. She…liked Simon. I certainly cannot blame her for that. Desperation makes people do things they might regret later."

She glanced once more at Simon and found he was looking back at her at last. She was drawn in immediately. How many times had he stared at her across how many rooms just like this? And she had stared back, telling herself that he only saw her in friendship, that her own feelings were just fleeting foolishness that would fade if she tried to ignore them hard enough.

None of that had been true. Now she understood better. Now she saw the longing in Simon's eyes, she felt it calling back to him from herself. She realized it had always been that way, their souls reaching out toward each other from whatever distance was between them. Her heart ached at the thought of it, of what they'd almost lost, of what they'd had to sacrifice. And it ached because she wasn't certain Simon would ever allow himself to be happy because of that sacrifice.

"You do not deserve censure," Idlewood said softly.

She looked up at him once more, surprised by his words and the gentler tone with which he said them. "No?"

"As I said, it is more complicated, isn't it?"

She nodded and then motioned her head toward Simon. "And what about him? Does *he* deserve censure?"

Idlewood lowered his gaze. "Did Crestwood tell you about our encounter in the billiard room?"

She stiffened. "Simon has not spoken to me tonight. I had no idea you'd had some kind of argument. But I have eyes—I can see how you look at me, at him. There are sides being taken here, aren't there, in your circle of friends? And *you* are separating yourself from Simon."

"There were other ways for what has happened to happen," Idlewood said. "Ways that would have been less damaging. But—"

He cut himself off and Meg stepped closer. "But?"

"Perhaps I shouldn't have been so harsh to him. Crestwood is abusing himself enough for both of us. For all of us."

Meg winced. Yes, that was exactly what he was doing. Punishing himself for what he had done, for who he had betrayed. She looked at Simon again and found he was still watching her. And in that moment, she knew what she had to do. Reach out to him because he did not feel worthy of doing it first.

He needed comfort and she wanted to comfort him.

"Thank you again, Lord Idlewood," she said with a smile. "Will you excuse me?"

He nodded once and she left him, her heart racing as she moved across the floor toward her future, her best friend, her destiny. And prayed that he would let her in, even a little, and give her hope that they could someday be happy together.

CHAPTER 12

Simon knew he shouldn't stare at Meg across the room, but he couldn't help it. He'd never been able to stop himself. Now, though, she stood with Christopher, and from their expressions it was obvious they were engaged in a serious conversation.

After Kit's anger in the billiard room, Simon could only imagine what was being said. And he deserved all of it. His heart lurched as Meg said something to the earl, then began to come across the room toward him.

Simon had spent years telling himself to resist this woman. But how could he when she glided through the crowd, her gaze focused solely on him? She was beautiful beyond his capacity for description. And she was his. But only because he had stolen her out from under someone he loved like a brother. Because despite whatever else had happened, he *did* love Graham.

But he loved Margaret more. That had been all that mattered in the end. That had guided all his selfishness.

She reached him, unaware of his roiling, troubling thoughts, and smiled. That smile lit up the world, lit up *his* world. "Will you dance with me, Simon?"

He stiffened at the request and the impression it would leave.

Them looking happy and light together seemed a cruel slap in the face to Graham.

"Is that a good idea?" he asked.

Her smile faltered, and she swallowed hard before she said, "We've always danced before, Simon. Always."

He shook his head. "And look where it has gotten us."

Now there was no smile anymore, just a flash of pain and struggle. "Are you determined to be so miserable with where we are?"

"How can I not?" He glanced around the room, at all the eyes that were subtly or blatantly on them. "Look at them staring and judging and whispering. Look at the strain on James's face as he leaves the dancefloor with Emma. They should be happy and instead they must now deal with this. Look at the way I've betrayed all our friends. You talked to Kit—he must have stressed his disdain to you just as much as he did to me."

She shook her head. "Actually, he did not. Idlewood told me he regretted whatever words were said between you earlier tonight. And he feels, as I do, that you are punishing yourself enough."

He wished that were true. It didn't feel true. It felt like he should suffer.

"Please don't refuse me," she whispered, and took his hand.

Meg smiled, not the bright, glowing smile she had displayed when she approached, but something soft. Gentle. Something that was for him, only him. He was drawn into it, drawn into her, just as he had been for years. If it was wrong then, he hadn't cared. He'd still felt it even as he fought it.

He'd lost the fight in the end. When she looked at him that way, he would always lose the fight.

She seemed to sense that and wordlessly led him to the dancefloor. He put his arms around her, shivering as his hand splayed across her hip, his fingers folded around hers so intimately. He wanted her, so very desperately. Touching her had never made that easier. Now that he'd tasted her, taken her, it was even worse.

They swung into the steps, silent as she kept her gaze focused on his. He couldn't escape the dark brown depths—he drowned in them as always. For that moment, it was only the two of them in the world. Adam and Eve, meant for each other, but brought down by temptation.

That temptation had its price. But as he held her so close, he recognized it also had its benefits. After all, he was holding the woman he loved. In a week, he would be married to her. What he'd always wanted, he would get.

"I have a new riddle for you," Meg said.

His fingers tightened against her hip and he smiled down at her. For nearly the entire time they'd known each other, he and Meg had challenged each other with riddles, though in the past year they hadn't played their game. Not since the answer to one riddle he presented to her was love. After that, the game hadn't seemed as fun.

"We haven't shared a riddle in a long time," he said.

Her expression brightened. "I've been saving this one. Would you like to hear it?"

He nodded. "Challenge away, my lady."

"My first descends from yon eternal skies," she said. "And caused you and me lot of trouble, but that part doesn't rhyme. A winged weapon from my second flies. And in the whole these colors may be seen, yellow and blue, as well as red and green."

He pursed his lips as he considered her words. Then he cocked his head. "A rainbow?"

She laughed. "Indeed, it is a rainbow. Good show, Simon."

He felt his shoulders relax as they fell into their usual rhythm together. In that moment, the dance felt like old times, her smile like old times. They were friends, as they always had been and the drama that followed them presently didn't feel so painful.

The music ended and he executed a quick bow before he took her arm and began to lead her from the dancefloor. For the first time in a long while, he had a bit of hope.

And then they passed by a small group of attendees. From

behind a fan, he heard hissing tones and saw glares as the two of them made their way off the floor. His heart sank, taking with it all his good thoughts. When he looked at Meg out of the corner of his eye, he saw her cheeks flaming red. The glisten of tears in her eyes.

All his fault. He couldn't pretend this wasn't his fault. Or that the consequences weren't real and powerful. When he came near her, he hurt her. That was just a fact, even if he didn't want it to be true.

"Simon," she said, turning toward him.

He shook his head. He loved her. He had always loved her. But James had been right in choosing someone else for her. Simon had never been good enough for her, and he still wasn't.

"Excuse me, Meg. I must go," he said, then turned away from her and left the ballroom as quickly as he could.

Meg stared as Simon left not just her side, but maneuvered his way toward the exit of the ballroom. When they'd danced, she'd felt a connection to him. It hadn't just been that renewal of their friendship that had occurred when she told him her riddle, but something more. He'd stared down into her face and she'd seen his heart in his eyes. She'd seen something deeper than friendship, more potent even than desire.

He'd let the connection stand, she'd felt him lean into it and into her. And then the crowd had whispered and he flinched away.

She clenched her fists and stepped forward, knowing everyone in the room was watching and not giving a damn about it. She followed him, ten steps behind as he departed the ballroom. She followed him up the stairs. She followed him to his chamber.

He was so distracted that he clearly had no idea she was behind him. He was shutting the door to his chamber when she reached out and caught it, pushing in behind him before closing the door. She reached back and locked it as he turned and stared at her, eyes wide. But also filled with wanting.

Her body responded to that wanting and her hands began to shake at her sides.

"You should not be here," he whispered, his voice rough and husky.

She lifted her chin. His desire for her was the only weakness he allowed himself. The only way they could be close without him putting up barriers created by his guilt. Perhaps one day making love to her would allow him to feel something deeper for her.

It might be her only path to the future she so wanted.

She moved forward and wound her arms around his neck, lifting up on her tiptoes to kiss him. He muttered a curse against her mouth, but then drove his tongue deep inside, pushing her back against the door with all his weight and pinning her there as he ravished her with deep, desperate kisses.

"You should not be here," he panted again, but his hands bunched her gown, lifting it inch by inch as he slid his mouth down the side of her neck.

She pushed at his jacket, tossing it on the ground behind him before she lifted her hands to the complicated knot of his cravat. His fingers grazed her bare thigh and she gasped with the sensation of his warm hands on her naked skin.

He froze at the sound, staring down at her with war in his eyes. Then he stepped away and her heart sank.

"You should not be here," he said for a third time, this time his voice quiet and low. She expected him to force her out, to turn away.

Instead, he unbuttoned his shirt and cast it away with his jacket. Then he reached out and stripped open the buttons on her gown with just a flick of his wrist. He tugged her dress and chemise down together, and suddenly she stood before him in naught but her stockings and slippers.

He shook his head slowly as he looked her up and down, leaving her wondering how he judged what he saw. This man who could have and had had anything he wanted from women. Was she good enough? Desirable enough?

The answer came when he unfastened his trousers and revealed the hard length of his erection. He kicked away his trousers and leaned in, caging her against the door and brushing his lips back and forth against hers.

He drew a breath as if to speak again, and she lifted her hand to cover his lips. "But I *am* here, Simon."

"Yes, you are," he whispered, then caught her hips in both hands and lifted her.

She latched her legs around his waist, clinging to his shoulders to regain her balance. He smiled as he pushed her hard against the door and then thrust, sliding inside of her with one smooth motion.

She gasped at the invasion, so different from the last time when there had been pain. Tonight there was only pleasure, intense and instant. She ground her hips out of instinct, and that pleasure multiplied.

His eyes shut and he let out a long breath before he began to pulse into her. Deep thrusts that always ended with a perfect circle of his hips so he hit her clitoris on each movement.

"Oh God," she murmured, her vision beginning to blur as everything in her world became focused on the place where they were joined.

He pressed harder, faster, watching her face with intensity, changing his rhythm when her expression changed, keeping her ever on the edge of release but never letting her fall completely over. This was pleasure, but it somehow also felt like punishment. As if he were showing her how he could give or take away, how he could make her want to beg for him.

If it was meant to make her question her decision to come to him, it didn't work. She lifted into him, rubbing her bare breasts against his chest as she drove her tongue into his mouth. She tasted mint, whiskey, some other sweet essence that was just Simon and

JESS MICHAELS

nothing else. She was drunk with it all, and that was when he let her fall.

Three perfectly timed thrusts and her body erupted with the pleasure she'd been seeking. Her hips jolted against his, her inner muscles rippling against his hardness.

"Christ, you test me," he murmured, setting her down at last and separating their bodies.

She stared at his still-hard cock, glistening from her slick release, and then looked up at him. "You aren't going to—to—"

"To come?" he finished for her, giving her a name for what had just happened. "Oh yes, Meg, I'm going to come. After you do again."

She caught her breath. Her legs were already shaking from what had just happened and her entire body felt spent and relaxed. She didn't think she could take a second round of such intensity.

"Can I...do that?" she asked, her voice shaking as hard as her hands.

He caught her waist and dragged her forward, tight against his hard body. "That sounds like a challenge. And that means you come two more times before we're done."

"Simon—"

He cut her off with a hard, driving kiss as he hauled her across the room. He released her in front of the full-length mirror in the corner of the room. She blushed as she stared at herself, hair still perfectly done, but utterly naked and trembling from release.

He grabbed a chair from in front of the fire and placed it before her, its upholstered back to her front. The chair blocked some of her view of herself, but there she still was with Simon looming up behind her in the reflection, his naked body nearly touching hers.

He caught her hands from behind and guided them to the back of the chair, gently closing her fingers around the top. "Hold on," he ordered, his tone thick with desire. "And watch. You think you can't take more? I'll show you that you can."

She caught her breath at this new side of the man who would be her husband. Simon was dangerous now, and yet she was anything but afraid. His driven desire was something she craved, not dreaded.

He positioned himself behind her, lifting her hips slightly before he spread her open and slid easily back inside her waiting body. This new position, combined with watching him curled over her, knowing that he was taking her, made her body flare with new and more powerful pleasure.

Her eyes widened as he began to thrust into her, hard and fast. He was hitting some place inside of her, some hidden place that felt just as good as when he touched her clitoris. She clutched at the back of the chair harder, staring at his straining face, mesmerized by her own parted lips and wanton movements of her body as she arched back to meet his thrusts. This was animal and lustful and oh, so very perfect.

He cupped her breasts from behind, lifting them, teasing the nipples as he watched them writhe together in the mirror. She dipped her head back, resting it against his bare shoulder as he continued to take her.

He let out a low moan and then caught one of her hands, gliding it away from the chair and down between her legs. He pressed her fingers against the slick nub of her clitoris and massaged there. Pleasure shot through her and she bucked against him.

"Just like that," he whispered against her ear, thrusting harder now as he released her hand and left her to touch herself without his help. She ground down against her clitoris and back against his cock, reaching, reaching until for the second time her body spasmed in pure release and ultimate pleasure. This time it felt even more intense and she barked out a cry as she watched herself come in the mirror. Watched him as he made her come, a wicked smile tilting his lips.

Her pleasure had only just faded when he slid out of her and turned her into his arms. His mouth ground against hers, sucking her tongue, swirling his own around it. He pulled away and turned around the chair where he'd been taking her. He gently pushed her back until she sat, staring up at him in pleasure and confusion and utter surrender to anything and everything he would ever want to do to her.

He dropped to his knees before her, opening her by draping each of her legs over the chair arms. He dragged her forward to the very edge of the chair and met her gaze as he lowered his mouth and began to lick her. Her body was only just coming down from the edge of her previous two orgasms and his tongue swirled over her clitoris, taking her right back to the harsh edge between pleasure and pain.

She drove her fingers into his hair, pushing him in, rising like a wild wanton against his tongue and finding orgasm so quickly that her body nearly shook off the chair. He pressed his hands into her hips, holding her steady as he forced her pleasure further than she thought she could survive.

He watched her as she came the third time, and as her tremors faded he lifted her from the chair edge, pushing into her body as he carried her to his bed. He rested her against the edge and held her gaze as he stroked hard and fast just a handful of times. His face twisted and he growled out her name as he spilled his hot seed inside of her.

For a moment, they remained like that, bodies joined, him bracing himself over her, staring down at her. Then his eyes widened and his stare shifted. Almost like he had been caught up and now he truly saw what he'd done.

"Simon?" she whispered.

He stood up, backing away. His face was pale as paper. "I'm sorry, Meg."

"Sorry?" she repeated as she gingerly lowered her legs and found she could, somehow, still bear her own weight.

"I treated you like a common—" He cut himself off. "This is what happens with you. I lose all reason, all sense."

"If that is losing reason, I am all for it," she said with a shake of her head.

"But look what it does. You heard them whisper, Meg. You know the cost."

"Simon..." she began.

He raised a hand, turning his face away from hers. "Don't," he murmured. "Please don't, Meg. I'll—I'll leave you to dress. To...fix yourself. I'm sorry."

He said nothing more, but turned and strode through the adjoining door to his dressing room. She heard the key turn in the lock once he was gone and was left staring at the barrier now between them.

She was upset that he'd left her, of course. Every time he turned away it stung. But there was also hope inside of her. Simon was fighting a war inside of himself. A war that, if she won, might mean they could be happy.

So she picked up her chemise from the tangled mess of her gown on the floor, and went about planning for their next skirmish.

"I plan to win, Simon," she said as she shimmied the thin fabric over her head. "I plan to win."

CHAPTER 13

M eg stood at the window, staring down over the drive. Below, James, Emma and her mother were bidding their guests goodbye, signaling an end to the country party that felt like it had begun a lifetime ago. In some ways, she supposed it had. So much had changed since it began.

She shifted position and groaned at the ache in her muscles. That was a reminder of the passionate encounter with Simon after the ball the night before. Somehow she had forced herself to return to the ballroom after she cleaned herself up. To pretend that it hadn't happened even as she thought about it constantly.

Simon had not done the same. A fact that had caused a good many whispers through the crowd. She was certain the fact that he had not yet been seen by anyone this morning was also going to be a topic of conversation in many a carriage on the way back to London.

She sighed. "It seems the nightmare never ends," she murmured.

Behind her, she heard a throat being cleared and turned to find Simon standing in the doorway. His face was pinched but otherwise unreadable, and she had no idea if he had just heard her words or was just troubled by her presence in general.

"I'm sorry," he said. "I didn't mean to disturb."

He turned as if to leave the room and she held out a hand, moving toward him cautiously. "Oh, please, don't go."

He remained half turned from her, his face only in profile. His eyes shut and she saw that war within him again. That war she had to win.

"Meg," he whispered, pleading in his tone.

She ignored it and kept moving toward him. "Simon, can't we pretend for a moment that we are still friends? Please, won't you just forget the engagement, forget what we've...done together last night or before."

He flinched. "You ask the impossible. I can't do that."

"Please," she repeated, reaching his side at last. She took his hand gently, feeling him stiffen when she did so. If he wanted to pull away, she did not allow it, tightening her grip. "For a moment when we were dancing last night, we both felt that connection rekindled."

"And then the world made its comments, Meg. Are you going to tell me you haven't had cruel remarks slung at you because of me?"

She thought briefly of the unpleasant encounter between herself and Sarah Carlton the night before, but shook it away. "Well, no one is going to say anything now. It's just family left in the house, Simon. Please, come sit with me. Be my friend. I need one right now and I think you do, too."

The war waged on, and finally he looked down at her and she saw this battle, at least, was won. "Very well."

She smiled and all but dragged him to the settee. She practically shoved him into place and took the seat at his side. She leaned in to pour tea, sweetening his just as he liked it before she handed it over and prepared her own cup.

"What do you want to talk about?" he asked, his tone strained.

She could see he feared her broaching the topic of their engagement or their wedding or, God forbid, their *marriage*. A part of her wanted to talk about all three of those topics.

But today was about their friendship, so she smiled as if none of the hard things existed and said, "Did you see Sir William Hargrave in the garden yesterday?"

Simon shook his head. "I don't think so. What was he doing?"

"Well, you know his eyesight is failing, and I've been told on good authority that he has spectacles but refuses to wear them. He's vain as a peacock."

Simon had begun to smile. "On good authority, eh?"

"Very good, but I shall not reveal my sources," she said with a laugh, her heart feeling light as they once again fell back into the kind of playful, easy friendship they'd shared for so many years.

"Protect the sources, it's of utmost importance, I agree," Simon said, and sipped his tea. "So we have a half-blind Sir William in your garden, I assume without his glasses."

She nodded. "Yes, and it was getting late in the afternoon so the shadows were beginning to draw out over the shrubbery and the statues that are placed between them."

"Yes?" he encouraged, drawing out the word.

"I overheard talking as I was picking some fresh flowers for the arrangement in the foyer and I went toward the sound only to find Sir William having a long discussion..." She took a dramatic pause. "...with *Venus*."

Simon barked out a laugh. "He was talking to James's half-naked statue of Venus? The one you used to drape cloaks around and put hats on?"

"To be fair, I was hardly more than a child when I dressed her up," Meg said with a laugh of her own. "I'm surprised you recall that at all."

His face got a bit more serious. "I recall all of it," he said softly.

Her heart beat a little faster at his words, at the increased intensity of his gaze when he said them, but forced herself to remain light.

"Well, Sir William would have likely enjoyed Miss Venus in all her finery, for he was having a full conversation with her. He hardly drew breath," she said with another giggle. "I considered stopping him and explaining, but he was having a lovely time. And I didn't want to embarrass him."

Chuckles shook Simon's frame and he tilted his head back. She stared at him, enthralled by seeing the Simon she'd always known and loved, right here with her again.

"Of course you're too kind of correct him. Poor man, I wonder what he thought when his lady friend didn't speak or accompany him back inside."

She shrugged. "That she was a good listener? Or playing hard to get? Either way, I assume they will be wed before the year is out."

The last sentence stopped Simon's laughter short and seriousness entered his face again. Meg frowned. Apparently her words about a wedding reminded Simon of their own rapidly approaching one.

"I suppose you and I have no place to laugh about anyone else's behavior," he said slowly. "Not after what we did."

She pursed her lips, loath to leave behind the comfort she had once again found in this man's company. In fact, she refused to do so.

She set her teacup down and met his eyes, arching her brow in challenge. "Are you speaking of the scandal created by Lady Margaret and the handsome Duke of Crestwood?"

Simon's brow wrinkled and he stared at her. "What are you doing?"

"Of course, is it so unforeseen that they might find themselves in this predicament?" She leaned in conspiratorially. "After all, they have been close for *years*."

His frown deepened as understanding dawned. "Margaret—"

"Come, don't be coy, Simon," she said. "You *always* have a unique take on all the day's gossip. What is it on this situation?"

He cleared his throat, and for a moment she thought he might just get up and run like he had been running for days. But then he sighed. "I think some would say that the duke is a cad and should have been called out by Lady Margaret's former fiancé or her brother. Men have perished in duels for far less than what he did."

Panic gripped Meg at even the thought of such a thing. That Simon would have been willing to fight, to die, over the slights he had caused Graham and her brother. And that it was only the decency of those two men that had kept a calling out from happening.

She forced herself to take a few calming breaths before she said, "I suppose some would *also* say that Lady Margaret should have been sequestered to the countryside, shunned forever by good Society and even her own family."

Simon's eyebrows lifted. "Some would say she made that very suggestion, herself."

She smiled, though the memory of that awful day in James's office did not make her happy in the least. "That may be true. But I think all those people would be wrong, regardless."

"Oh?" he said. "Then what do *you* think?"

She scooted a bit closer, letting their knees brush against each other. Even that benign swish of fabric on fabric made her ultra-aware of her desire for so much more.

"I think," she whispered, lifting a trembling hand to brush it over his smooth cheek. "That Margaret and the duke are simply human. That people make mistakes, especially when they're desperate."

His face flashed with a moment of sadness. "You think it a mistake?"

"The way it was done, perhaps." She leaned in, letting her breasts rub his arm, tilting his chin down toward her. Their lips nearly touched when she added, "But I'm not sorry, Simon. I wish you weren't either."

He stared down at her, tension still coursing through his body. But then he cupped her chin and brought his lips to hers. The passion between them pulsed there as he tangled his tongue with hers, as he pulled her closer, almost into his lap. But there was something else in the kiss. Something deeper than mere desire. Something she felt and wanted to hold on to with both hands.

His mouth moved over hers, gentle at first, but with increasing passion as she wound her arms around his neck. He tilted his head, driving his tongue between her lips as the world around them faded and all that was left was powerful physical sensation and driving lust.

Meg was almost swept away by it. She could feel Simon close to the same when there was a soft sound from the doorway to the parlor.

They jerked apart, both turning to find Emma standing in the entryway. Her cheeks were flamed and she was staring up at the ceiling as if there were something interesting to be found there as she said, "Oh, hello, you two. I was wondering where you were."

Simon lunged to his feet, backing away from Meg as he shook his head. Once more the wall he had been putting between them was slammed down and he gave her a formal bow before he said, "Excuse me, ladies. I think I should…go."

The last word was strangled, and without further explanation he slipped past Emma and disappeared from view.

Meg got to her feet slowly and walked over to the window. For a long while she stared out, and eventually she watched as Simon strode from the house and walked out over the rolling hills of the estate, away from the gate and down toward the woods.

She couldn't help but make a frustrated sound in the back of her throat. Emma said nothing through it all, but at last Meg heard her close the parlor door. She turned and found her friend leaning back against the barrier, watching her intently.

"You have no one else to talk to about this," Emma said. "I know that's isolating when things are so…*complicated*. Will you tell me what is going on?"

Meg bent her head. "I've been reticent to discuss the situation with you because of your marriage to my brother. I know that you two don't keep secrets."

"You fear I'll run to him, telling him anything I hear?" Emma asked.

"Wouldn't you have to?"

"Well, I don't recall that promise in the vows we made when we wed," Emma said with a laugh. "I admit that we are honest with each other. We went through too much individually and together to be less than that. But honesty doesn't require that I tell him every detail of every conversation I have. And I think James would want you to have a friend in this difficult place you find yourself. Only if I felt you were endangering yourself would I feel it was necessary to discuss our private exchanges with your brother."

Emma's words were comforting and Meg adored her so much. The idea of sharing the truth with a friend was tempting indeed.

Still, she was cautious as she said, "If it won't put you in a difficult position."

Emma moved forward and took her hand. "You and I are friends. I want to help. Talk to me."

"Simon..." she began, and then it was like a dam burst and all her words spilled out, rushed together. "Oh God, Emma, he *hates* himself for what he did to Graham. What he did to James. What he did to all his brothers in their club. I know people see him as somewhat shallow, I think because he's so quick to laugh or tease, but that isn't true."

"No, all those who truly know the man recognize his depth," Emma said. "He feels deeply."

Tears stung Meg's eyes as she nodded. "He does. And right now he is bent on self-punishment. On keeping himself from happiness because he feels he doesn't deserve it. I have no idea where that will lead us."

Emma nodded slowly. "James has said something similar. That Simon's personality is to punish himself for every wrong. But we know where this leads, Meg."

"Where?" Meg asked, and she was terrified of the answer.

"A wedding," Emma said with a small smile. "It's all leading to a wedding, isn't it? Let it lead there and see if that changes the situation."

Meg swallowed hard. "But what if it doesn't?"

"Then you'll deal with that when that comes." Emma squeezed her hand gently. "You can do it, I know you can. Things weren't easy for James and me, either. You know that. But we're here now. Happy. Strong in our knowledge that we love each other and that we will work to make our love stronger every day. It takes work and dedication and understanding, but it's worth it. And I know you'll commit yourself to the same path."

"But will he?" Meg asked.

Emma blushed again. "He certainly seems to have a passion for you, if what I walked in on is any indication."

Meg shook her head as memory after memory bombarded her, from the passionate kiss in the cottage on the night that had started all this to the heat of his touch the night before when he'd claimed her pleasure over and over.

"Passion," she said with a shiver. "Oh yes, there is that. He allows *that* if nothing else and it's the only hope I cling to, the only way to make him surrender a bit of himself to me."

"Am I to assume you two have…" Emma waved her hand to indicate the obvious.

Meg smiled despite the difficult topic. Regardless of the fact that her friend's passion for her own husband was obvious as anything, Emma was not comfortable saying certain things out loud. Even in private between friends.

Meg hesitated. "We truly didn't do anything that night in the cottage when everything was blown apart, Emma. He kissed me once, but it went no further."

"Of course you didn't," Emma said. "I never believed otherwise. I'm not sure James or even Graham did, either. But obviously things have now changed."

"Simon and I have circled each other for years," Meg whispered. "It was all friendship and light, but beneath the surface we both knew what we didn't admit. That there were deeper feelings and longings that could never be pursued."

"But now they can," Emma said.

Meg nodded. "At least the longings. Simon refuses to address the feelings. But the moment we were engaged, he swept in and all that passion, all that desire, it overflowed."

"And how do you l-like it?" Emma stammered.

"It is wonderful," Meg admitted with a sigh. "So different than some describe it. There is no bearing or suffering through it. I am an equal partner in my pleasure and his. And there is so much pleasure."

Emma smiled, and the knowing light in her eyes let Meg know she understood completely. "I'm glad of it. You deserve that kind of connection. And it is a good sign. If he allows that passion, it means he may one day allow the rest."

"That is my hope, too. I know I cannot keep the desires of my mind and the needs of my body separate. I can only hope it's the same for him. Perhaps someday I can help him realize that keeping a wall between us won't change what we did. It will only keep us from ever being happy."

Emma slipped an arm around Meg's waist, and they looked out the window together, silent as they both pondered the secrets that had been shared between them. Meg did feel better having told someone the difficulties in her heart.

But nothing had been resolved. And she knew she still had a mighty fight ahead of her if she wanted her future to be as settled and happy as Emma and James's had become.

CHAPTER 14

S imon caught his breath as Meg stepped from the house and took her place beside him on the grand staircase that led from the drive. She was exquisite in a dark green gown that was cut not scandalously low, but low enough for his imagination to take flight.

Of course he'd *seen* her in the past five days. They'd shared meals and passed in halls and engaged in casual conversation with her family. But they had not been alone together since their encounter in the parlor the morning the other guests departed. Nor had he been afforded the chance to go to her room or have her join him at night.

He supposed he could pretend it was because both of them were very busy with preparations for the wedding that now loomed up the next day. He and James had been wrangling the special license and preparing other formal documents and settlements. He knew Meg and Emma had also been involved in a flurry of activity, if the constantly scurrying servants and the never-ending stream of seamstresses traipsing in and out of the house with bolts of fabric had been any indication.

But he had a sneaking suspicion none of that was why he hadn't had a moment alone with Meg. Emma had seen the passionate exchange between them in the parlor. He had to believe that all this activity was arranged in part to keep them from surrendering to desire again before their official vows were taken.

So he ached for her as she took her place beside him. He ached to touch her. To kiss her. To feel her body against his. Oh, he wanted to take her, of course he did, but more than that, he missed her company. That quiet connection that had always been so easy between them but now felt so impossible and out of reach.

In that moment of realization, she looked up at him with a faint smile. "Simon."

"You are beautiful," he said softly.

Her lips parted in surprise at the compliment, and guilt stabbed him. It seemed there was no winning in his current situation. Either he maintained a distance in penance for his bad acts and hurt Meg, or he moved in close and took what he wanted without regard for all he'd destroyed.

He frowned and faced forward again, watching as a carriage thundered through the gate and came up the long drive and into the circle before them. The seal on the carriage door was his own, the Crestwood name represented by a flourished C surrounded by carved rearing horses and golden filigree, and his throat closed as a footman raced to open the door and help down the arrival.

His mother stepped from the carriage in a burst of perfume and disdain. She looked up the stairs, her gaze flitting over the others and settling at last on Simon. Her eyes narrowed and her lips thinned, and he felt her loathing as sharply as he ever had.

She moved up the stairs and started her greetings at the opposite end of the line, going first to the Dowager Duchess of Abernathe. He could hear her words drifting toward him, apologies for the mess Simon had put them in, regret for all the trouble, vague congratulations to Emma and James, even as she sniffed when she looked Emma up and down.

At last she reached him and Meg. Meg lifted her chin as the

Duchess of Crestwood glared at them. "And here you two are," was all she said.

"Welcome, Your Grace," Meg said, holding out a hand that his mother ignored.

Simon stiffened, frustrated that her disregard for him would clearly stretch out to his future bride, as well.

"Mother," he said.

She sniffed once more and turned to the others. "I am parched from that awful drive. May we retire to a parlor for some tea?"

"Of course," Emma said, motioning to Grimble as she and James led the way into the house. "Please, follow us."

The Duchess of Crestwood sharply turned her back on her son and moved to walk with the dowager, leaving Meg and Simon alone on the stairs. He let out a great sigh before he held out an elbow for Meg.

She remained facing him instead of taking it, her face lined with understanding and empathy. Of course she had known his mother a great many years. She knew some of the history that caused the strife that still existed between them.

"She hasn't forgiven you?" she asked softly.

He tensed and turned his face, not looking at her as he said, "No."

She reached up, cupping his cheek to turn his gaze back to her. Slowly, she lifted to her tiptoes and brushed her lips across his. Every other kiss between them had been passionate, driving, possessive, desperate. This was something else. As she pulled back with a shy smile, his heart swelled with all the things he knew he shouldn't feel.

She slid her hand into the crook of his elbow and tugged him forward. "Come, we face her together."

He did as she commanded, allowing her to lead him into the house and down the hall to the parlor where the others had gone. He said nothing, but he wondered at her gentle strength, her solidarity with him in that moment. He'd had no siblings growing up.

He'd felt like he had no family at all until he met James and Graham and they'd started their club with all the rest. That was part of why his betrayal was so bloody awful.

But entering the parlor with Meg, feeling her presence and her support as his mother turned another glare his way, this felt like something deeper than mere family.

This was the possibility of true partnership, of never being alone even if they were apart, because their souls were united as much as their bodies and their lives. And that was thrilling and terrifying all at once, for he knew he didn't deserve such a bond.

He broke away from Meg gently and moved to the sideboard where Emma was already holding out a cup of tea for him. He forced a smile to his mother and said, "I am happy you have arrived in time for the wedding, Mother. I thought you might join us sooner —was my letter delayed?"

The duchess arched a brow, the cruel line of her lips tilting in a nasty half-smile. "It was not. I just saw no need to rush over to celebrate this humiliation you've brought on us. And as for what you *thought*, I have *thought* a great deal about you, my boy. Would you like me to recite all the *thoughts* I've had?"

He flinched not only at the harsh cruelty of her words, but at the way every other person in the room shifted with discomfort at witnessing her set down. Everyone, that was, except for Meg. She rushed forward, smiling as if nothing had happened, even as her eyes snapped with defensive anger on his behalf.

"Your Grace, why don't you sit? You've had a busy day. I'll bring your tea," she said. "Two sugars and milk, yes?"

The duchess appeared surprised that Meg knew that and nodded. "Yes, just so. Thank you."

His mother moved away from Simon to a place before the fire and settled in for a conversation with the dowager as Meg and Emma prepared the rest of the tea. Simon walked away from them, crossing the large room to stand aside at the window and observe.

It took James less than thirty seconds to break away from the ladies and join him. Simon refused to look at his friend, but continued to watch Meg handle his cranky mother with grace and kindness. From time to time, she glanced up at him, meeting his eyes with a purpose, with a message that she was his ally.

And she was more than that, in truth. She was his best friend. She had been for what seemed like forever, far more than even James or Graham had ever been.

"You all right?" James asked at last.

Simon still didn't look at him. "Oh yes. My mother has despised me for years, as you well know. Now she just has a larger group of people who agree with her assessment of my poor character. It will make her happy to have so many who see me as a failure as a man and a friend."

James stepped in front of him, forcing Simon to look at him at last. James's jaw was set hard, his eyes lit with emotion. "*I* don't despise you," he said softly.

Simon caught his breath. Since the scandal that had started all this, he and James had not spoken of what he'd done. He'd been avoiding the topic, truth be told, for he didn't want to hear James say he hated him. He didn't want to lose one of the people he loved most, especially since he'd already lost Graham and who knew how many others in their circle.

But now James held steady in his regard, making his position as clear as the window that overlooked the garden behind them.

"No?" Simon asked.

James slowly shook his head as a response.

Simon wanted to hold onto that answer with both hands. He wanted to take it and feel that he deserved it. But then he thought of Graham's crumpled expression before he left, of the way he had broken himself not just from Simon and Meg, but from James and the others.

"After I destroyed your friendship with Graham, ruined your sister and damaged your family name, you *still* don't despise me?"

"No," James said firmly.

"Well, you should," Simon whispered.

"You despise yourself enough for both of us," James retorted.

Simon was ready to respond, but before he could, his mother rose to her feet. "I would like to retire."

He sighed and stepped forward. "May I show you to your chamber, Mother?"

She looked him up and down, then shook her head. "No, thank you. I prefer to have Grimble do it. Good afternoon."

Simon clenched his teeth as she left, hating how the rest of the room, his friends and his future bride, all stared at him, pitying him when he deserved censure, not understanding. He let out his breath in a burst and said, "Excuse me."

Without waiting for a response, he left the room, running from what he felt, what he wanted and what he knew he should not have.

Meg stood on a wooden box in the middle of her chamber, holding perfectly still as the seamstress made a few last adjustments on her gown. In less than twenty-four hours, she would don it to become Simon's wife.

This was an event she had often pictured, especially after her betrothal to Graham. In fact, sometimes the fantasy of her wedding gown was the only thing about that marriage that she had actually looked forward to. And today her mind wasn't on it at all, despite how beautiful the dress was, with its pale pink silks, creamy lace overlay and the hand-stitched pearls that danced along the skirt.

"May I ask you a question?" Emma asked as the seamstress excused herself to fetch some additional fabric from her carriage on the drive.

Meg nodded. "Of course."

"When the Duchess of Crestwood arrived today, I expected her to be…"

"Different?" Meg asked, clenching her teeth as she thought of her future mother-in-law's nasty behavior. She'd forced herself to be kind in order to ease Simon's discomfort, but what she'd wanted to do was slap the duchess across the face.

"Yes," Emma said. "Why is she so cruel to Simon?"

Meg sighed heavily as she stepped down from her perch and crossed to the fire. Memories mobbed her, including one strong one of Simon standing in the stable six years ago, tears streaming down his face as he tried to process his father's death. She had held his hand—it was all she could do.

"Simon's father wasn't like ours," she said at last. "Not abjectly cruel. He ignored Simon, though. Utterly ignored him. Nothing he could do ever brought him attention. Good marks in school, good behavior, bad behavior, all of it was for nothing."

"He must have longed for connection," Emma said softly, her hand straying to her stomach, as if to shelter the baby inside of her from such cruelty.

Meg nodded. "And he found it, with my brother and their club full of friends." She sighed. "Part of why he is so devastated by his role in the breaking of his friendship with Graham, I think."

"And his mother was the same as his father?" Emma asked, returning to the original subject.

"No, she has always been all about appearances. Looking to be the perfect family, the perfect duke, the perfect everything." Meg folded her arms. "But when Simon found acceptance with his friends, he stopped seeking it from his father. He spent holidays with us, not them. Just before his father died, the duke sent Simon a letter. It was horrible, filled with demands." She winced. "Simon didn't answer. His father died shortly thereafter and Simon did not go home for the burial."

"The duchess was angry," Emma said with a sad shake of her head.

"That service was to be one of her finest moments, with all eyes on her in her loss. I'm sure she had it planned perfectly, from every sniffle to each twist of her handkerchief," Meg said, unable to keep the disgust from her tone. "And instead she had to spend it explaining why her son was not there. Of course, it was because Simon was *here*, trying to process the death of a father he'd never truly had. But she's never forgiven him."

Emma sighed heavily. "Well, that certainly explains a great deal about Simon."

Meg wrinkled her brow. "Like what?"

Emma shrugged. "Well, the past few weeks aside, he is never serious. When he's with others, he often pretends that he has no depth, though it's obvious that isn't true. And he doesn't...*fight*, even for what he wants or believes in."

Meg flinched. That last observation hit so very close to home. Simon had *never* fought for her.

"A-And you think that is because of what he experienced as a child?" she whispered.

Emma nodded. "We all carry our past with us, don't we? I know I do. James did for many years, and even now when the weight is lighter, he still holds it on his shoulders. Simon is no different. I can imagine if he spent his life never receiving his father's attention or meeting his mother's impossibly high standards, it would make him reluctant to try to win anything."

Meg pondered that. She'd never thought of it in those terms before. "I suppose you're correct. Pretending to be easy and satisfied at all times would be easier than striving for what was unattainable."

The seamstress returned then and Meg stepped back into place as Emma changed the subject to something less personal in front of the stranger. But Emma's words rang in Meg's head.

It was possible Simon was incapable of fighting for what he wanted. But if he didn't, she wasn't certain she would be able to fight hard enough for both of them.

CHAPTER 15

Simon had been married for eight hours. Though the service was small, with only the vicar and their families in attendance, somehow the day had still stretched long. He and Meg had never been alone, dragged from one duty to the next.

But now, as they stood in the parlor, after-dinner drinks in hand, Simon was beginning to see a light at the end of this very long tunnel. And the light was going to bed…with his wife.

He shivered at that thought, of having her after so many days apart. Of having her when she was truly his and he was truly hers. There was meaning in that, even if he wanted so desperately to deny it.

James was talking, and for the first time in several moments, Simon actually took in the words coming from his friend's mouth. "—back to London in two days," James said.

Simon blinked. "I'm sorry, I must have been woolgathering. Why return to London so soon?"

Emma tilted her head and her gaze slipped between him and Meg. "James believes that returning to London as a family group, rather than hiding in the countryside, will show the world that we give full-throated support to your marriage. It will encourage acceptance no matter what level of scandal remains."

Simon pressed his lips together. He could well imagine the level of scandal was high, indeed. Unless someone else did something truly horrifying, he and Meg would be the topic of conversation for what was left of this Season and likely all of the next.

"We must go on with life," Meg said, her tone falsely bright. "I agree that a return to London will give us the opportunity to do so."

She shot him a glance and he caught his breath. They were married. When they returned to London, she would move into his townhouse in the city. They would truly live as man and wife.

He cleared his throat and tried to find some focus. "Yes, well, I suppose it is all we can do. Now I find I'm very tired. It was a long day."

Meg set her drink down and moved toward him. "I'll—I'll join you," she said, her cheeks flaming a little.

He swallowed hard and offered her an arm. Together they said their goodnights and then he guided her toward the parlor door. They had only taken a few awkward steps toward the staircase when his mother stepped out of the room behind them.

"Simon," she said.

He turned, drawing Meg with him and barely contained a sigh. The now-Dowager Duchess of Crestwood looked just as sour and judgmental as she always had. This was clearly not to be a supportive moment between them. Not that he could recall one from before, either.

"Yes, Mother?" he ground out, focusing as much as he could at the gentle feeling of Meg's fingers against his arm. They were tightening a fraction now, a buoy against what was to come.

"Because I have little choice, I shall support you as best I can in public," the dowager said. "My going against you will only make it harder for *me*."

He shook his head slightly. "Well, I'm sure Meg and I appreciate the support no matter for what reason it is given."

He moved to go, and his mother snapped, "I am not finished." Meg tensed at his side as they returned their attention to the dowager as she continued talking. "You have always been a disappointment, Simon, so I ought not to have expected more from you in this. But I want to be perfectly clear that my public support in no way reflects a private sentiment. Your ridiculous decision to act on your heart rather than with your head shows me what kind of fool you are. Straighten up, or you shall lose all your allies. Including me."

Simon gritted his teeth. He'd heard some variation of this speech from her over the years. Today it hit home, for he remained raw over all he'd done to bring them to this place. He opened his mouth to reply when Meg slid her hand from his arm and stepped forward.

"Your Grace, Simon and I are infinitely aware of all the damage we have done to ourselves and those around us, both socially and in terms of emotional damage. No one needs to tell us, for aside from the Duke of Northfield, I do not think anyone is suffering as much as we are. Not that you offer comfort, but there we are."

"Margaret—" his mother began, her eyes flashing.

Meg held up a hand. "*I* am not finished. The fact is that Simon will need support, not just publicly, but privately, as we work through this difficult time. If you are not equipped or inclined to provide it then I offer a solution: stay away from us."

His mother's lips parted and she gasped in a breath that seemed to echo in the hallway. "How dare you? What right do you have to speak to me in such a way?"

"I married your son today," Meg all but growled. "Which makes *me* the Duchess of Crestwood now, and responsible for the appearances we choose to uphold. I will make myself clear—if you ever again speak to my husband in the manner you just did, I will cut you out of our circle so fast, you will not know what happened." Meg smiled, but it wasn't the usual warm and welcoming one that graced her lips. "You and I can be allies, or we can be very public enemies.

It is your choice. But choose wisely, for I know how much appearances mean to you."

They all stood for a moment, both Simon and his mother shocked by Meg's statement. At last, the dowager stepped toward him. Simon tensed, ready for another attack or set down or demand.

Instead she met his eyes. Her nostrils were flaring with upset, her eyes flashing with anger, but to his utter shock she said, "I apologize, Simon. I spoke out of turn. Of course you have my full support."

Simon could only stare. In all his years on this earth, his mother had never apologized to him. He had certainly done so to her dozens of times, but never had that act returned. Now he hardly knew what to do.

Not that it bothered Meg. She gave another tight smile and leaned in to kiss his mother's cheek. "Thank you, Your Grace. Now my husband and I will retire. Come along, Simon," she said, taking his arm again and turning him toward the stairs.

He followed her, almost blindly, his ears still ringing from what had just happened. What she had said and done.

The fact that she had championed him, which no one had really ever done in his life. As they reached the door to his chamber, he turned toward her.

"Meg," he whispered.

She lifted her face to his, dark eyes clear and focused on him. He caught his breath, knowing she was his and still hesitant to let that be.

"Thank you," he murmured.

"For what?" she asked, lifting a hand to touch his face.

He shook his head. "You know what. What you said to my mother."

A shadow crossed her expression. "I know it was speaking out of turn and normally I wouldn't be so blunt, but I am tired of the way she treats you, Simon. And I will not stand for that in my house, not while I am duchess."

He couldn't help but smile. "You have been duchess all of eight hours and already you lay down your rules."

She nodded and reached around him to open his chamber door. "I do. Now come inside and we can—"

She cut herself off and he turned to look at whatever had caught her attention in the room. When he did, he caught his breath. The chamber was lit with dozens of candles, there were flowers adorning each table, and a fire burned. There was a bottle of wine at the table next to the bed and two glasses.

Meg shook her head. "Emma."

Simon lifted his brows. "You think so?"

"Yes." She moved into the room, walking around to smell the roses closest by. "This will be the first time we've done this where we weren't sneaking around."

He shut the door behind him and turned the key in the lock slowly. "Yes. And since all the other guests are gone and my mother has been put in a chamber on the family side of the house, no one will be able to hear us, either."

She turned to look at him, her eyes now lit with desire. "That sounds very promising," she whispered.

He frowned as reality began to edge in. "Meg," he said.

She moved to him in a few long steps. "Stop," she ordered. "You will have a lifetime to tell me how wrong this is. How terrible you feel. How much we deserve to suffer. Tonight, just touch me. Please."

She caught his hand as she spoke and gently lifted it, pressing it to her breast as she maintained focused eye contact. He looked at his fingers against the lacy pink gown, closing them around the globe of her breast beneath. Her breath caught and he smiled.

"Are you seducing me, Your Grace?" he asked.

She nodded. "Indeed, I am, Your Grace." She turned her back to him. "Now unfasten me."

His hands shook as he lifted them to the tantalizing row of tiny buttons that ran from the top of her gown all the way to where her bottom swelled beneath the fabric. One by one, he loosened them, his fingers fumbling in his haste to see her without the beautiful dress. His fingers brushed her chemise beneath and she jolted like an electrical charge flashed between them.

He smiled as he leaned in and gently kissed her neck. "I feel it too," he whispered.

She rested her head back against his chest, pushing her body into his, grinding her backside ever so slightly against his cock. He caught his breath, for she was quickly becoming versed in what he liked, how to make him wild with desire. Of course, she always had, without even trying. Her effort only made it more intense and powerful.

He stripped the last few buttons open, but before he could push the dress off, she stepped away from him. Facing him, she met his eyes as she slowly shimmied one arm free, then the other. The silk glided down, inch by inch, until she was free of the dress and stood before him in just her chemise.

He could hardly breathe. The undergarment was the same soft pink as the gown, but it was so thin it was almost sheer. He saw the shadow of her hard nipples beneath and the triangle of her sex even lower. With a shuddering sigh, she pushed the chemise from her body and stood before him naked. He froze, just staring, just taking her in and reveling in how beautiful she was.

"Take off your clothes," she ordered, her voice shaking.

He arched a brow. Somehow he'd never pictured Meg taking control like this. But he found he liked it. He watched her as he shrugged out of his jacket, then lifted his hands to his cravat, untying and unlooping the long sash of white silk until it dangled from his fingers.

"I have an idea about what to do with this," he whispered.

Her pupils dilated. "So do I."

He found himself grinning despite the heat between them. "What would you do?" he asked.

She swallowed. "You're too…big."

He wrinkled his brow. "You stopped complaining about that almost immediately, if I recall."

She rolled her eyes, but she was laughing and suddenly everything was easy between them again. Even this. "Not your cock, Simon. You. It's too easy for you to take over when we do this. And I want to…explore. So I suppose if you gave me that cravat, I would use it to tie your hands so you *couldn't* take over."

His eyes went wide at that idea, that Meg would be so bold as to tie him to the bed to have her wicked way with him. It was almost too erotic to bear. Slowly, he moved forward and looped the cravat over her, draping it down around her waist. He tugged, drawing her forward with the reins he had created.

When she was flush against him, her body trembling in his arms, he whispered, "Then do it."

He leaned in to kiss her, drinking of her lips for what felt like an eternity. Then he stepped away and lifted the cravat up to her neck, leaving it there, the tails hanging down over her breasts and all the way to her thighs.

Seeing her dressed in only that thin scrap of silk made his cock throb. He made quick work of his shirt, then leaned on the bed to remove his boots and trousers.

When he stood, she caught her breath as she stared at him. "I shall never get used to seeing you like that," she murmured. "Not for a hundred years."

"I hope not," he teased as he backed toward the bed. "I always want to see that look of pure adulation on your face when you see my hard cock."

Her eyes went wide and then she laughed. The musical sound filled the room, and once again everything was easy between them, as it had been in all the years they had pretended to be just friends.

In that moment, he saw how beautiful their marriage could be. Or could have been if it had not started so very badly.

But he didn't know how to repair it now. How to fix what was already done. How to make what they'd done be acceptable in any form.

"Stop thinking," Meg whispered with a slow shake of her head. "And get on the bed."

He stared at her closely. "How do you know I'm thinking?"

"I know you. And you're getting a wrinkle in your forehead. Just...let tonight be about this and us. The rest will come, the rest will be faced as we get to it."

He said nothing, but did as she asked and climbed onto the bed. He settled onto the pillows and smiled at her. She was right that tonight he didn't need to think. Everything would come rushing back tomorrow just as it always did. Tonight he wanted to steal this moment, to make her his wife in every way.

Tomorrow he could suffer the consequences. As he should.

"Now you have me, Your Grace," he purred. "So what exactly will you do with me?"

Meg's mouth felt very dry as she stared at Simon, naked on his bed, waiting for her, watching her with a half-smile on his face. In that moment he was her whole world, her whole heart, her everything.

And she wasn't ready to say that, so tonight she had to show him. This was the only way he would surrender to her, so she had to use that against him. She had to use passion to open his heart.

But when it came to seduction, she had very little knowledge to go from. Her statement that she'd tie him down to allow herself the freedom to explore had been said in haste, and now, in a little more leisure, she regretted it.

"You have the cravat," he said gently. "So tie me up."

She nodded as she came across the room. She grabbed one end

of the cravat, hissing out pleasure as she dragged the silky fabric across her skin to remove it.

His eyes widened. "Better do it fast, Meg, or I'll do exactly as you fear. I'll flip you onto your back, tie *you* down with it and make love to you until you're weak from me."

She swallowed, for that kind of punishment didn't exactly sound like something she wanted to avoid. But she still leaned in, looping the long white tie around his wrists again and again until his hands were pressed together. She still had quite a bit of length left in the cloth, so she looked around for what to do with it.

The bed had an elaborately carved headrest, one with little grooves and holes in the dark surface. Without hesitation, she darted the ends of the cravat through a hole and tied the ends firmly, leaving him tied to the headboard.

When she stepped back, she found him staring up at her. His cock had somehow gotten harder as she did her work and his breath was short, making his toned stomach lift rapidly. "You are a natural," he growled. "Now you have me, so what will you do?"

Her hands shook as she lifted her fingers. "Take my hair down," she whispered.

He chuckled. "So it is to be torture. I can handle torture."

"I hope so," she teased as she glided her fingers through her elaborate hairstyle and brought pins clattering to the floor around her. Long locks bounced around her bare shoulders as she did so and he stared at it all, licking his lips like she was a treat he was about to savor.

She felt the same way, of course. Staring at this man, this powerful man, now tied to a bed and laid out for her pleasure, she was almost overwhelmed by what she could do. The freedom she had to play any game she wished.

The power of that was both heady and terrifying.

"You can't do anything wrong," he reassured her, as if he could read her mind just as she could read his. "Just do what you'd like."

She crawled up next to him on the bed, emboldened by his

suggestion. Being with him, it had always been him taking and her receiving. Now she wanted to take. She wanted him to receive. She leaned over him, her hair falling across his chest, and kissed him.

He made a soft sound in his throat and opened to her, holding back as she tasted him, traced his tongue, invaded him as she had been invaded so many times before. She felt the coiled tension of his body as he allowed her to rule the kiss, she saw it in the way his hands fisted against the lightly tied knot. She was under no illusion that he couldn't just rend the fabric in two and have his way.

That he didn't was a gift, and she knew it.

She eased down his body, tasting his throat, letting her hand slip over the angles of his collarbone and lower to his chest. Her mouth followed the trail of her fingers and she reveled in the taste of his hot skin, the way his muscles bunched beneath her tongue, and his breath caught.

Giving him pleasure was better than anything, and suddenly she knew exactly what she wanted to do to him. She lifted her gaze up his body as she stroked her tongue over his nipple, repeating an action he had taken so many times before. His body arched and she smiled.

The test proved her theory. What pleased her also pleased him. And that encouraged her as she dragged her mouth down his stomach, over the ripples of his muscles there. When she moved even lower, he lifted his head and stared at her.

"What are you doing, Meg?" he whispered, his voice rough and raw with desire.

She smiled as she brushed her lips against his hip. "When you kiss my sex, the explosion is so powerful. I want to test if it would be the same for you."

He grunted out a curse she'd never heard before and struggled to sit up. "Meg, you don't have to—"

She ignored him as she wrapped her fingers around his cock and stroked him gently. Now that she'd had him fitted inside of her more than once, now that she'd felt the pleasure that act could bring, she did not fear him anymore. She was simply fascinated by the thrust of him. By the silky feel of his skin. By the hard steel it covered.

She leaned in and darted her tongue out to trace just the head. He responded by flopping back on the bed, his hips lifting toward her of what seemed like their own accord as he let out a bark of incoherent pleasure.

"It seems the answer to my theory is yes," she whispered, and licked him again, this time swirling her tongue around him slowly.

He pushed up, his cock passing her lips briefly, and her eyes widened. While he'd licked her with his tongue when he pleasured her in this way, he would likely find his pleasure differently. After all, when he was pulled into the warm, wet cavern of her mouth, it was very much like thrusting into her sex. That would be what would give him release.

She gripped the thick base of his cock and wrapped her lips around him, drawing him in as deeply as her body would allow before she withdrew. He twisted below her, his eyes coming closed as he let out a ragged sigh that told her everything she needed to know.

She repeated the action, rubbing her tongue against his thick length as she did so over and over. When he moaned, she marked it. When her speed changed, she tested his reaction. Slowly, she began to learn his pleasure and the fact that she could make his legs shake, his heels dig into the mattress, was pure power.

"Meg," he gasped at last. "God's teeth, I'll spend."

She lifted her gaze at him with a smile. "That is the goal, isn't it?"

"Not tonight," he grunted. "Tonight I want to be inside of you. Please."

Her eyes went wide at the *please* and she gently released his cock to stare at him. His face was taut with pleasure and tension, his eyes wide with both pleading and hot desire.

And on their wedding night, she couldn't deny him any more than she could deny herself. She moved back up his body, kissing the same trail she had followed on her way down. When she reached his lips, she kissed him deeply as she positioned herself over him, straddling his lap, for that seemed the best way to take him.

He shifted, and she could see him wanting free of his bonds again. His arms strained, the muscles tight and his knuckles white from gripping fists against the fabric. She wanted those hands on her. She wanted him fully.

"If I untie you," she asked as she brushed her lips against the harsh line of his jaw. "Will you flip me over on my back and take over?"

"Is that what you want?" he murmured, his voice dark now, dangerous.

She shook her head. "No. Well, yes, of course that would be lovely. But I want to...to..."

"Ride me," he suggested.

She lifted her head and stared down at him. "Yes. I've already been claimed. Tonight is my turn to claim you. Will you let me if I untie you?"

He nodded, the movement jerky and swift. "I will."

She leaned forward to unloop the cravat, her fingers fumbling with the knots she'd tied. He grinned up at her as she fiddled and he tugged hard, rending the fine silk apart and sending pieces of it fluttering around them on the bed as he freed his hands.

"My valet will despise me for that," Simon said as he sat up, wrapping his arms around her. In this position they were now face to face and she shivered at the intimacy she so longed for. Intimacy of spirit as well as body.

"Do you care?" she whispered.

"Not a bit." He angled his head and kissed her. She let her arms come around him and held tight, memorizing the sleek strength of his body, feeling his cock hard and ready between them.

At last he lay back, sliding his hands to her hips. "I promised I wouldn't dictate this. So tonight I'm yours, Meg. Take what you want."

She caught her breath. *Hers.* How she wanted it to be true, but she feared it wasn't. The passion between them often felt completely separate from the rest. But she would still try, she would never give up on making this man her husband in every way she had secretly fantasized about since she was little more than a girl.

She shifted, reaching between them to align their bodies. When she glided him into place, taking him inside of her the first few inches, they both shuddered in pleasure together. When she flexed her hips, he slid easily to the hilt and she shut her eyes briefly. His fingers tightened against her skin and he rocked her gently.

Now her gaze flew open at the riot of sensation that rocked through her body. He grinned and said, "Yes," in answer to a question she hadn't the power to ask out loud.

She moved with him as he guided her, rolling her hips, grinding her pelvis to his and drawing him deeper and deeper until she couldn't find a place where she existed and he didn't. Pleasure built in her as she took him, pleasure in her body, pleasure in her very soul, and judging from the twisting tension on his handsome face, he was finding the heights of it too.

And then she was soaring, flying off the edge of a terrifying cliff as her body rocked with release and she cried out his name. He sat up once more, one smooth motion, and dragged her mouth to his as he lifted up into her. He grunted out her name against her tongue and she felt the hot spurt of him inside of her as he crushed her sweaty body to his.

They remained like that for what felt like a blissful eternity, legs and arms tangled, bodies intertwined, his mouth brushing across hers. She clung to him, joy swelling in her that they could have this kind of connection, a glimpse of a future that she so desperately wanted.

But at last he drew back, staring into her face just inches from his. And she saw the transformation from a man who was wrapped up in passion to the man who would put walls between them.

But he didn't get up. He didn't abandon her. He simply wrapped his arms around her and held her against his chest. She clung to him, tears stinging her eyes, hope swelling in her chest. She was too afraid to speak, lest the spell be broken and so she just lay there, as her eyes got heavier and her breath got deeper until sleep stole her fears.

~

Simon stared down into Meg's face, as beautiful when she was relaxed in sleep as it was when she laughed or talked. Now he knew that. Because she was his in every way. And yet, he didn't feel unfettered joy at that fact. When he looked at her, he saw Graham's crumpled expression, heard his friend's harsh voice. He saw the damage he had done.

The feelings washed over him and overwhelmed him. Gently, he set her aside and got up. He stoked the fire and then grabbed for a robe that was draped across the settee near the bed. As he covered himself, he heard her catch her breath.

"What are you doing?"

He squeezed his eyes shut. He hadn't wanted to have a confrontation with her tonight of all nights. He hadn't wanted to let her see just how broken he was by what he'd done. But now it felt unavoidable.

"I think it might be best if I slept elsewhere," he croaked out.

There was a long hesitation and the next time she spoke her voice was strong. "We are married, Simon."

He took a deep breath and faced her. She was sitting up now, her body covered by the tangled sheets. Her expression was unfiltered though. Pained and full of fear. He hated that he did that to her.

"Yes, I was there," he whispered, thinking of his happiness in that moment where they were declared man and wife. Where they could never be parted again. Except by his own tangled emotions.

She shook her head. "You tease without any joy in your tone, but you know what I'm saying. You and I are bound now, by the law and in the eyes of everyone in Society. It cannot be undone."

"What do you want from me, Meg?" he asked, more frustrated with himself and the situation than with her. "You seem to think that now that we've said vows, it erases the past. But it doesn't. Right now Graham is back in London, despising us both. Anyone who attended the party is telling everyone who will listen about the scandal, which means you and I will enter a firestorm that will perhaps leave your reputation in tatters. Am I supposed to smile about that? Pretend that both those things aren't true, just because I—"

He cut himself off and she pushed to her feet, going to him without a thought for her nakedness in body or in spirit. "Because you what?" she pressed.

He stared at her and swallowed hard. "Because I want you."

How much more he wanted to say. How he wanted to tell her the rest. That he loved her and had always loved her. That he wanted the chance at a future, but that the idea of it made him despise himself. And that he feared that he would fail her even more than he already had.

She reached for him and he dodged her hand, stepping toward the door to the adjoining chamber.

"Please don't," he said softly.

Tears filled her eyes. "Why? Must you be determined to destroy yourself?"

He was silent for what felt like forever and then he said, "I have destroyed everyone else, Margaret. Why shouldn't I also burn in this fire I created?"

He said nothing else, nor did he wait for her reply. He just turned away because he could no longer hide from her. And what he had to show was nothing short of monstrous.

CHAPTER 16

Simon stared straight ahead as his mount clopped along the road. Less than forty-eight hours after his wedding, and he, his mother and the Abernathe family were all headed back to London and the uncertainty of what would face them there. Behind him, the carriages rumbled and he did his level best not to look back.

He could have been riding with his wife, but he had elected to travel on his horse instead. He had expected Meg to argue, but her crumpled face and soft acquiescence had been harder to take than if she had asked him flatly to join her.

"Are we going to talk about anything?"

Simon stiffened as James trotted his horse up next to him and fell into step. There was no avoiding this, it seemed. Perhaps it was better to simply deal with it now and have it done with.

"I'm surprised it's taken you so long to ask me," Simon said, keeping his eyes on the road rather than dare look at his friend of over a decade.

James shrugged. "I was waiting so that you would have an opportunity to talk to me. Or better yet, her."

Her. There was no doubt the *her* James referred to. Simon forced himself to look at James. "I talk to her."

James rolled his eyes. "Please don't sport with whatever small level of intelligence I have, Simon. I have eyes and I can see what you're doing."

Simon clenched his jaw and tried to keep his tone calm and unbothered. "And what is it you see?"

"You're avoiding her. Even if I didn't know you two slept in separate chambers last night, I would be able to see it from the way you act in public."

Simon flinched. The separate chambers hadn't actually been his idea. He had waited for his wife to join him last night in the room they'd shared after their wedding. She had never come. At last he had gone to look for her and found her in her own bedroom, asleep, tracks of tears on her cheeks in the firelight.

Self-hatred burned within him at that memory.

"I-I don't want to talk to you about that," Simon said.

James jerked his face toward him. "And nor do I wish to discuss my sister's habits with her husband, but I am left with little choice. Meg's future and her happiness are important to me. As are yours."

Simon caught his breath as he turned in his seat to look at James. There was nothing false to his friend's expression. He looked frustrated, perhaps even angry, but he didn't hate Simon, even though that was exactly what he deserved.

"*Mine* shouldn't be," he said softly.

James's jaw tightened. "So you insist on punishing yourself?" he asked.

"I deserve to be punished."

"And you will punish Meg in the process," James snapped. "Damn it all to hell, Simon, haven't you destroyed enough?"

Simon returned his attention to a spot on the horizon.

James sighed. "Look, you want to hate yourself, fine. You want to destroy your relationship with me, apparently I can't stop you. But I swear to God, if you destroy Meg..." He reached and out and grabbed Simon's shoulder, making him look at him. "There will be hell to pay, Crestwood."

Without breaking their intense stare, James lifted his fist to indicate the train of vehicles and animals should stop. As everyone did so, he swung down from the horse.

"I'm going to ride inside with my wife and my sister for a while," he said, "to afford you the opportunity to think about what I've said. I suggest you do so, Simon. I understand why worthiness is such a challenge for you. I knew your father, I've spent time with your mother. I even understand why you hate yourself for Graham. But you are on the precipice of making a terrible mistake. One that you will not come back from. Think hard about what you want to do or you'll find yourself losing *everything*."

When Simon said nothing, James walked away, tossing the reins of the horse to a footman who had scurried from the top of the carriage and would now ride the horse for a while. Simon knew his friend was right.

He just wasn't certain how he could accept the future that had been given to him and atone for the past all at the same time. Until he figured that out, he couldn't be a husband to Meg or a friend to James. He certainly couldn't be a friend to himself.

So he was left to his own mind, which was currently a very dangerous place to be.

Meg stepped into the foyer at her new home in London and drew a deep breath as she faced a line of smiling servants, ready to greet her. Of course she knew some of them already. She had come to Simon's townhouse so many times over the years, accompanying James when he called. She had all but memorized the rooms. She knew what chair was Simon's favorite, she knew how he always arranged his desk just so.

"Welcome, Your Grace," the butler, Finley, said as he stepped forward to take her wrap and Simon's hat and gloves. "We are so pleased to have you home."

She smiled as she was introduced along the line to the rest of the staff. All seemed genuine in their greetings and none reflected any hint that they might have heard gossip about their new mistress. Of course, she knew they had. Something so big as the compromising position she and Simon had found themselves in would ripple not just through her world, but the worlds of servant and merchant alike.

Which did not help her with Simon in the slightest. It was partly why he withdrew from her. Him and his damned penance.

"Your Grace, I know you and the duchess had supper at the Duke of Abernathe's after your arrival in London," Finley was saying as the other servants drifted away back to their duties. "But may we provide any dessert or drinks?"

Simon glanced at her and she shook her head slightly. He smiled at the butler. "Thank you, Finley. As much as we appreciate the offer —and I know Mrs. Giles would likely whip up something very tempting if we asked—I think Her Grace and I are simply too tired from travel to partake tonight."

Finley nodded. "I understand, sir. Of course, ring if anything changes. Otherwise, your chamber is prepared."

Simon lifted his brows and Meg felt there was some kind of silent communication going between the men. "Fully prepared?" he asked.

Finley smiled again. "Yes, Your Grace."

"Good man, thank you," Simon said, nodding once more as the butler bowed his goodnights and left them alone.

Simon offered her an arm. "Let me show you to our chamber."

Meg shivered as she touched him. *Their* chamber. Actually, his room was one of the few in this house she had never seen. She wondered what it would look like, as well as the duchess chamber that would be adjacent.

She didn't have to wait long to find out. He guided her up the stairs and to the end of a long hallway. It was the last room where he drew her through elaborately carved double doors. She entered into an antechamber that was entirely masculine and very Simon. It had gray walls with stark white accents and a large fireplace where two chairs faced the bright flames. She tilted her head as she stared at one of them, a sunny yellow armchair that looked very familiar and very out of place in his space.

"Is that...is that my chair from my room at my mother's home?" she asked, spinning on him briefly before she moved over to look at the piece.

He smiled. "Yes."

She jerked her face toward him. "What in the world is it doing here?"

"Well, I spoke to your maid and asked her what needed to be arranged to be brought from the house to make you more comfortable here. She mentioned how much you enjoyed reading in your favorite chair, so when I wrote to my servants to make the arrangements for our return, I asked that it be fetched. James and your mother agreed, and here it is."

Her lips parted, and she stared at the chair and back at him. "You did this for me?"

Discomfort crossed his expression. "Yes," he said softly.

She moved to him, but he took a step back and motioned his hand toward one of the closed doors on either side of the antechamber. "Come, I'll show you your room."

She swallowed hard, moved by his kindness, frustrated by his withdrawal. "Very well."

He opened the door and allowed her to pass through first. She caught her breath as she did so. The room, which she had expected to be stark and plain after years of no use, was instead bright, sunny and painted in her favorite shade of welcoming yellow. Flowers sat on the table before a mirror, but they were not just any flowers. They were lady's glove, a purple bell flower that she had always adored. Amongst their buds were arrays of sweet honeysuckle, so the room had a warm and welcoming scent.

"You—this cannot be how the room was before I came," she said. "Because these are all my favorite things."

He nodded. "As I said, given the circumstances, I wanted to do all I could to make you comfortable. Happy."

She stepped to him again and this time he remained in place, even though she saw his gaze slide toward the door. She caught his hands before he could manage some kind of escape.

"Thank you," she whispered as she lifted up on her tiptoes and pressed her lips to his.

He groaned and his arms came around her, crushing her to his chest as he drove his tongue into her mouth. She felt his desire, but also his desperation as he pushed her back into the room and up against the edge of the bed. His hips ground into hers and the hard ridge of him pressed into her belly, lighting a fire in her that only he could quench.

Though as much as she wanted this, the fact that it was the only thing he would give her freely was still troubling. As if he sensed her thoughts, he tore his mouth away and stepped back, hands shaking.

"I'm sorry," he panted.

"Why?" she asked, straightening and smoothing her wrinkled gown.

He shook his head. "It was a long day of travel. I know you're tired and I should not—"

"I'm not made of glass, Simon," she said softly. "And the only thing we have truly established in this marriage thus far is how compatible we are when it comes to sex."

His eyes went wide at how blunt she was.

She shrugged. "Don't look so surprised. I can say what I see as easily as anyone else. You want me. I want you."

"You're a lady and—"

"I'm your wife. And I have needs that you fulfill. As I hope I fulfill yours," she said, her mind spinning back to what James had said about Simon's proclivities weeks ago. She still wasn't certain what to think of that bawdy past she was not meant to know about.

He turned away. "There were no invitations waiting for you, Meg."

She wrinkled her brow at his change of subject. It only served to heighten her uncertainty about satisfying him. But she wasn't ready to address that just yet.

"What are you talking about?" she asked. "We didn't ask Finley if anyone had left anything for me."

He looked at her slowly. "Finley is as predictable as the sunrise each morning. Whenever I return home, he presents me with my invitations and correspondence immediately. If he didn't do so, that means there was none."

She shrugged. "We have only just returned and—"

"You are not invited to events because of me," he interrupted, his voice suddenly strained. "Because of what I did."

She pursed her lips, her frustration bubbling to the surface. "Because of *us*," she corrected sharply. "And what *we* did. You can try to pretend otherwise, but there were two of us in that cabin that night, Simon. And I was the one who ran off into the woods rather than deal head-on with the fact that I didn't want to marry Graham. I am just as much to blame for anything that happened as a result of my reckless behavior."

"You would not have taken off your clothes and spent the night in the cabin with me had I not suggested it," he said, folding his arms.

"And I would have likely frozen to death as I tried to walk home," she countered. "Would that have been a better solution?"

He flinched, and she saw the flash of pain and horror on his face at the idea. "No. No, of course not."

"This is not only your responsibility."

He was silent for a moment, and she prayed he was absorbing her statement. Perhaps even open to believing it.

But then he shook his head. "You say that now, Meg. But someday you will recall how much you liked being popular. And you'll hate me as much as *he* does for destroying your future."

He turned away then and left her, shutting the door behind him with a quiet click that felt like a gunshot through her breaking heart. She spun away, fighting to draw breath, and stomped her foot.

"*You* are my future, you great buffoon," she said.

She covered her face with both hands. Here she had everything she'd ever wanted. Marriage to the man she loved, a home, a room that was perfect, but it was all empty. Empty because she had no idea how to shake Simon awake and force him out of his fog of guilt and self-punishment.

And she feared her time to do so was running out.

CHAPTER 17

Meg tried to keep her chin up and a smile on her face as she stood in her brother's home the next day, but as Emma entered the parlor, all the bravery she'd been trying to portray collapsed under its own weight. As her lip began to tremble and her eyes filled with tears, Emma raced across the room to her.

"Oh, dearest, dearest," Emma cooed, taking her to the settee and waving off the servant who had come to inquire about tea. "There, there."

Meg buried her head in Emma's shoulder as great shuddering breaths racked her. "I'm sorry," she murmured at last, drawing away from her friend's embrace. "I should not have called when I am in such a state."

"Because you are in such a state, that is when you *must* call!" Emma argued. "I want to see you, to help you. You've been very brave in these past few weeks. You have earned a good cry and a place to be entirely honest. Now tell me."

Meg met her eyes. "Oh, Emma, we've talked about this before, I know, but I am at such a loss. I have dreamed almost my whole life of marrying Simon. Even when I was engaged to Graham and pretending to plan my life with him, I dreamed of Simon. It was wrong, I know, but utterly true. I have loved him since I was fifteen!"

Emma's expression softened. "I thought as much, even if you didn't say the specific words."

"But he is resistant to anything beyond what we share in his bed," Meg continued. "I'm sorry to be so blunt, but that is the heart of it."

Emma's cheeks had flamed, but she didn't look offended as she said, "I see. So he makes love to you but will not connect with you outside that realm."

"And it is utterly confusing," Meg said, rising to her feet and pacing the parlor restlessly. "When we are together…physically…it is wonderful. I feel all his passion for me, his desire, I feel that he cares. And I always wish, hope that when it's over he'll allow the connection to continue."

"But he pulls away," Emma said, a frown drawing down her lips.

Meg nodded. "He pulls away physically, but also he throws walls up between us." She stopped pacing and faced Emma. "I-I know that it is his guilt over the betrayal of Graham that causes some of it. But I'm beginning to wonder if there is…more to it."

"More?" Emma asked. "What more could it be?"

Now it was Meg who felt heat rushing to her cheeks. She moved to the door and shut it. She leaned against it and said, "The day James found us in the cottage…God, it feels like a lifetime ago…he and Simon were arguing, and he said something. He—he said that the reason he picked Graham for the betrothal to me was that Simon was whoring around London at the time. And he and the Duke of Roseford were, er, *sharing* women."

Emma's eyes bugged wide and her mouth opened and shut a few times. "Oh. My. I-I-oh…"

Meg nodded. "Yes, my response exactly. I'm not even certain how that would work."

Emma tilted her head to the side. "I suppose one of the men could be taking her while she sucked…you know, it doesn't matter. It seems like they were talking about something that happened a long time ago. As titillating an idea as it is, what does it have to do with you?"

"What if I'm not enough?" Meg whispered. "What if all his rejection, which he says is because of Graham, is really because he needs me to be more than what I am, than what I could ever be?"

Emma got up and moved to her, catching her hands. "Meg, you *are* enough. James occasionally makes noises about the trouble Roseford continues to get himself into around Town, but to be truthful, he has *never* said anything about Simon. If he was once less than prudent with the lovers he chose, if he was doing something wild, the time has passed for that. I don't believe for a moment that his problem is you not satisfying him. If you didn't, why would he have pursued you for sex the moment the engagement was announced? If he didn't want you, he would have waited."

Meg nodded slowly. "I suppose so. And I suppose when I think of the way he touches me, the way he kisses me, I know he does want me, even if he once desired something far more outrageous than I'm able to provide. But it doesn't make me feel better, because he still pulls away. He still refuses to have a true marriage or life with me. So what do I do, Emma?"

Emma stared at her a moment and a light came into her face that Meg had never seen before. Normally Emma was sweet, gentle, but there was a warrior fire in her expression as she grabbed Meg's upper arms and held tight.

"Fight!" Emma said with a little shake to Meg's shoulders.

"I have been, haven't I?" Meg whispered, for she had certainly been in many a battle with Simon since that night in the cottage.

"You have. But I know you've been going about things indirectly, haven't you? Being careful with Simon? Being understanding?"

Meg nodded. "Yes. I've been giving him his space."

Emma shook her head. "Then you must stop doing that. This has been a war of small battles, it may be time for a far larger one. Something more direct. Simon *loves* you—anyone who looks at you together can see it, even if he wants to deny it out of some misplaced sense of guilt. You have to force him into seeing that the future is where he must go, not live in the past."

Meg drew back, for Emma had just said the thing she longed for most. The thing she couldn't believe at the moment. "Loves me?" she repeated softly. "He has wanted me, cared for me, but he's never said the other."

"I know. Have you?"

She tensed. "No," she admitted softly. "I've been too afraid of his rejection. If he turned away, I think I would have to…to leave. I couldn't bear having him know that I loved him and him not care in the slightest."

"*That* is what fighting is," Emma said. "It's knowing that we might lose what we desire, but doing it anyway so that we can get what we need even more."

"Did you fight for James?" Meg asked, thinking back to earlier in the summer when her brother and Emma had circled each other. She hadn't ever believed their love was easy, but she hadn't considered that Emma was going into battle.

Emma smiled softly. "Yes. I misunderstood something I saw him do and my life became very clear in that moment. Despite everything my father was threatening, despite the danger posed to me by outside forces, I told James I didn't want to marry him."

Meg's mouth dropped open. "You did?"

"On the morning of our wedding, no less. I told him I loved him and would accept nothing less from him." Emma shivered, like even the memory still touched her. "It was *terrifying* to stand there, looking at him after I'd said those words, waiting for him to respond. I think that moment must have stretched out forever. But the risk was worth the reward. James didn't know how I felt. And once he did, it opened up a world of honesty and passion and love that has made everything else I ever went through fade in its intensity, replaced by contentment and joy."

"But what if James hadn't said he loved you?" Meg asked, trembling as she pictured Simon turning away from her.

Emma swallowed hard. "Then at least I wouldn't have lived a lie like my mother did or your mother did. At least I would have known how to proceed with my eyes wide open."

"I'm afraid," Meg admitted, her hands clenching and unclenching at her sides as all the worst outcomes of the bravery Emma described played through her head.

Emma nodded. "I know. But being brave is really about being afraid and doing something anyway. Be brave for yourself and for him. Whatever happens, at least you won't regret staying silent or passive about your own future."

As they stood together, Meg felt some of Emma's strength swirling into her and giving her what she lacked. "Yes, you're right of course," she whispered. "I've held back with Simon, as much as I've accused him of doing the same. I'm going to face him head-on. At this point, I think I must."

She let out a long breath and moved toward the parlor door. Emma laughed, "You are going right now?"

"Yes. Simon went to his club, but he should be back before supper. I think I'd best go home and make some preparations before he returns." She gave Emma one last look that she knew reflected her fear. "And before I lose my nerve."

Simon sat in the corner of White's, a drink in hand and a newspaper folded in his lap. He was meant to be sipping the drink and reading the paper, but neither was on his list at present. He was too distracted by thoughts of Meg and also by the chilly reception he had received since his arrival an hour earlier.

Oh, the men around him said hello, but no one had dared approach him and publicly declare they would remain a friend to him. Of course, he recognized he fully deserved that outcome.

Meg didn't. He did. But he would destroy them both socially thanks to his lack of decorum when it came to his feelings for her.

"Why did I follow her?" he muttered as he snapped the paper open and lifted it.

"My very question," came a slurred voice.

Simon froze, for he knew the voice as well as his own. He lowered the paper to watch Graham flop himself into the chair across from him. His friend's normally bright blue eyes were bleary with drink and he clearly hadn't shaved for a week.

Simon shifted, watching all the eyes on them from all around the room. In that moment, all he cared about was his friend.

"Graham," he said softly. "I-I didn't expect to see you."

"Should *I* hide away and let you have White's?" Graham snapped.

"No, of course not," Simon said, ducking his head. "There is no reason for you to hide from anywhere. You did nothing wrong."

A flash of raw emotion moved over Graham's face at that statement, but then it was gone. Only the understandable anger remained there, the disgust.

"Damn right," Graham muttered, downing the rest of his drink and setting it on the table between them.

"Would you like...would you like me to give up my membership here?" Simon asked.

Graham stared at him. "Not return to White's?"

Simon nodded. "If it would make it easier for you."

"Well, if we're talking about *easier*," Graham said, leaning forward. "Why don't you just leave London?"

Simon flinched. "I-I could do that."

"And that house we bought in Scotland," Graham continued.

"The hunting lodge?" Simon blinked. That was common property of all the men in their club. "We each own a part of that."

"You sell your part to me or to James," Graham clarified.

Pain ripped through Simon at the idea that he would be removed from his circle of friends. Because that's what selling his portion of the lodge would represent: that he was being removed from the club. He would lose *everything*.

"Very well, I can arrange that." Simon tilted his head, for Graham didn't seem to be finished. "What else?"

"What makes you think there's more?" Graham slurred, though his gaze was very focused now, almost clear.

Simon shrugged. "I know you. I know you value loyalty and what I did betrayed you. My penance cannot be so easy as this. What more do you need? What more do you need to take in order to balance the scales between us?"

Graham stared at him a long time. "Meg."

Simon stiffened. "What about Meg?"

"Maybe you don't prance around together, being a happy couple," Graham said slowly, his voice suddenly low and dark.

Simon paused. What Graham was demanding was exactly what Simon had already been doing, trying to distance himself from Meg as atonement for his sins. Now that Graham was actually asking him to do so, the reality of the request rang in his ears.

Meg was already skating on the edge with him. She reached out and he backed away, not because he wanted to, but because he felt he should. It wouldn't be very long before Meg would stop trying. She would be a fool not to. And then he would lose her.

So what Graham was asking for was for Simon to destroy his marriage. Finally and fully.

Before he could reply, Graham pushed to his feet. He wobbled slightly as he glared down at Simon. "You're a fucking coward, aren't you?"

Simon slowly rose, not to fight, but to defend himself if need be. Graham had always thrown a wicked right cross and one didn't want to be seated when it landed.

"I know I hurt—" he began, wanting to apologize. To help somehow.

"Goddamn it, Simon, don't fucking apologize to me," Graham interrupted as he shoved him hard.

Simon staggered but didn't move forward, even as the other men in the room began to circle toward them, wary but interested in this very public faceoff.

"What do you want me to do then?" Simon snapped, his patience fraying.

"Fight," Graham growled.

"I'm not going to fight you," Simon said softly.

Graham rolled his eyes. "Of course you're not. You never have. Not even for a woman you clearly love. You told me you love her, didn't you? But I mention that you should walk away from her and from friendships you've held for over a decade and you just...*sit there.*" He shoved Simon again, and this time the force drove Simon into the table. It tipped over sideways and both their glasses shattered on the floor.

"Stop," Simon ground out. "I don't want to fight you, Graham."

Graham tilted his head back and laughed. "I'd respect it more if you punched me in the mouth and told me that Meg was your wife and that was the end of it. I'd respect it more if you fought for *anything.*"

He shoved Simon one more time and this time it was enough. Simon set his jaw and pushed back as hard as he could. Graham moved like he'd come forward again, a grin on his face, but before they could actually come to blows, the others lunged forward. Arms grabbed for Simon, others caught Graham, and they were separated at last. Strangely, Simon regretted it. Perhaps a few punches between them was exactly what they needed to ease the tension.

"Go on," one of the gentlemen said, ushering Simon toward the door. "He's drunk and your being here only makes it worse. Go on then."

Simon edged to the door, but threw one last glance over his shoulder at Graham. His friend...or was it former friend...now had a bottle in his hand and he was offering loud toasts to uncertain futures as the others surrounded him, clearly trying to calm him down.

Simon frowned as he exited the club and waited for his horse to be brought around. He had always known he'd encounter Graham. They were both too prominent not to have that faceoff. But it hadn't been what he had expected. Graham was angry, yes. Graham was betrayed, one could see it written all over his face. Graham was even spoiling to fight.

But his challenge to Simon to actually take what he wanted and stop apologizing for it was unexpected. How could that be what Graham wanted after everything that had happened? Wasn't it spitting in the man's face to be happy and carefree with Meg?

He'd been telling himself for weeks that it was. And now he was left uncertain of what to do and how to proceed.

CHAPTER 18

Meg drew in a shaky breath as she looked around the master bedchamber one final time. It was perfect. Of course it should be, considering how much time and effort she had put into preparing it. Flowers were set around the room, a blazing fire brightened and warmed the space, the bedcovers were drawn back in the hopes what she would do would go well.

She turned toward the mirror. She was wearing her finest gown, and Fran had done her hair to perfection. What had Emma said to her before? That her clothing and her hair were her armor. Well, if so she was prepared for war now. She only had to wait for Simon and then somehow manage to say the words she had been rehearsing all afternoon.

As she paced her room, she tried to calm her racing heart. For years she had waited, loving Simon from afar, doing what she felt was right and best for everyone around her except for herself. Today she was taking the first step toward the future she wanted. With the man she loved.

And yet she had no earthly idea what his response would be. He *could* fall into her arms, surrendering at last to the feelings he had fought so hard and long to deny out of a sense of guilt and duty. She sensed that he wanted to do that. Or she hoped he did.

But he had such a strong sense of what he'd done wrong. Which meant he might put up a stronger wall than ever between them. One she feared she might never be able to climb, no matter what she did.

The risk was very high. The reward was even higher. And it was time, at last, to be brave. To fight this last fight and to hope that he would do the same. To think of her own wants and stop worrying about anything but her heart.

There was a light rap on the door and she jumped, as she faced the entrance. "Yes?"

The door opened and her heart sank. It was only Simon's butler.

"Yes, Finley?" she asked, trying to keep her expression serene. "Do you have word from His Grace?"

"No, Your Grace, not yet," Finley said, with apology lacing his tone. "He went to his club is all I know, I'm afraid there is no word from him as of yet. But you *do* have a guest, the Duke of Roseford."

Meg wrinkled her brow. Roseford had not sent word he was calling. "He came to see *me*?"

"No, to see His Grace, but since he isn't here…"

Meg nodded. "Of course, I'll be right down."

"Thank you, Your Grace. I'll tell him."

Finley left and Meg looked at herself in the mirror once more. She was in no mood to have company, especially not Robert. Thanks to James's slip of the tongue all those weeks ago, she knew Roseford had once been Simon's partner in debauchery. Who knew what he was encouraging her husband to do now?

She smoothed her skirts and made the short trip downstairs and into the parlor. Roseford turned from the fire when she entered, and he actually caught his breath when he looked at her.

"Roseford," she said with a blush. "I did not expect you."

He caught the hand she offered and lifted it briefly to his lips. "I'm sorry, Your Grace, I ought to have sent a card ahead, especially as it looks as though you are on your way out. You look lovely."

She smiled at his compliment. "Thank you. I am not going out, actually, I'm just waiting for Simon. He should be returning from his club shortly." A brief shadow crossed Roseford's face, and Meg's heart leapt. "What is it? Do you have news?"

"No, not at all. I-I actually came here looking for Simon, myself. You see, he isn't at the club."

Meg swallowed. "No?"

"No, when I arrived there a while ago, he had already left." Roseford shifted with discomfort. "It seems he—he encountered Northfield there."

Now Meg staggered and Robert actually reached forward to keep her from falling. He helped her to a chair and she drew a few breaths as she tried to remain calm.

"He and Graham saw each other. How bad was it?"

"A bit of shoving is all," Roseford said, his mouth thinning to a grim line. "At least this time."

She bent her head. "God, how I hate that their friendship is on such poor terms because of me." She sighed and stared at her clenched hands in her lap. "You saw Graham?"

Roseford nodded. "He was still there."

"And how…how was he?"

He hesitated. "Do you want the truth, madam, or some lie meant to comfort you?"

She jerked her face up at the faint disdain in his tone. She deserved it, after all, for the friendships between all the men in their club had been strained with her as the cause. "The truth, Your Grace. I am not some dainty flower who requires only positive words."

He arched a brow at her calm reply and she thought she saw a flicker of appreciation in his stare. "Very well. Graham is…troubled. Betrayed. He is not handling it well."

She squeezed her eyes shut as she thought of the pain Graham was in. "It's *my* fault."

He didn't deny that charge, but let out a long sigh. "We've all had our part in this debacle. *You* shouldn't have run off in a fit. Simon shouldn't have followed you that day. *I* should have made Crestwood leave the moment he said he wanted to—"

She stood up slowly and stared at him. "Leave?" she repeated as her entire body went cold and numb. "What are you talking about?"

Roseford's jaw set. "You don't know?"

She shook her head. "Know what?"

"I ought not say something if Simon hasn't."

She moved toward him, her hands clenched at her sides. "You're implying that my husband intended to leave, but you won't tell me any more details. You must understand that you cannot drop such an explosive accusation in my parlor and then walk away as if you did nothing. Tell me, Roseford. What do you mean that you should have made Simon leave? When did he *want* to leave?"

Roseford flushed and he refused to meet her eyes. His voice was taut when he said, "When you and Graham announced your wedding date, Simon came to me and we decided we'd go to Ireland. Or Italy. It didn't really matter where. He just wanted to go and not come back until after your marriage was performed. I thought he might have told you so himself, but it seems I've revealed a secret. One that will clearly hurt you both."

Meg's ears were ringing as she stared at the handsome man before her. Roseford was many things, and he had certainly never been her favorite of her brother's friends but he was not a liar.

"He was going to walk away," she whispered.

Roseford nodded. "You must see that was the honorable thing to do."

She clenched her jaw, her hands shaking as she stared at him. "Honorable. *Ballocks*," she finally choked out, "I'm so bloody sick of that word!"

Roseford's eyes went wide that she would curse in such a way, but before he could reply, Simon walked into the parlor.

"Roseford," he said. "Finley said you were here and—"

He cut himself off as his gaze slid to Meg. She knew what he must see, for she couldn't hide it. Her hands were shaking, her breath came short and tears filled her eyes no matter how she tried to angrily blink them away and keep her weakness from being revealed in such a humiliating fashion.

"Meg," Simon said, moving toward her. "What is it?"

"Roseford, get out," she whispered.

Roseford cleared his throat gently and bowed to her. "Of course, my lady. I'm sorry that I upset you." He moved toward the door and added, "And Crestwood, I'm just sorry."

Simon didn't acknowledge it as his friend left, closing the door behind him. "What is it?" he asked.

"You were going to leave," Meg said. Not asked—*said*, for she didn't want to give him a chance to launch into a hundred explanations of the unexplainable.

The color left Simon's cheeks and he stared at her in silence for what felt like an eternity. "Roseford told you?" he finally asked.

She nodded, but the movement felt jerky and unbalanced. "Yes. And thank God he did, for it seems you never would have. But that's what you're best at, isn't it, Simon? Withholding."

He flinched at the accusation and she could see that he wanted to move toward her. He didn't, of course. It seemed he was patently incapable of doing so.

"I wasn't trying to withhold something from you, Meg," he said softly. "I *didn't* leave, so I wasn't certain there was any point in telling you that it was my initial plan."

She moved toward him, hands clenched at her sides. "Do you wish you had?"

"Told you or left?"

"Left!" she cried. "Do you wish you had left?"

He bent his head. "If I had, I wouldn't have hurt anyone."

She drew in a sharp, hard breath and staggered away, recoiling just as she would have if he struck her. In some ways, it felt as though he had, for the truth of him...of *them*...now hung between them in a way she had been trying to hide from. Avoid. Pretend she could repair.

It was clear now that she had been a fool.

"You would have hurt *me*," she said, her voice hardly carrying.

He lifted his gaze slowly. "What?"

"Damn it, don't pretend that you don't know how I feel for you," she said with a violent shake of her head. "Don't pretend you didn't know all along. You and I have had a connection that went deeper than friendship, deeper than lust, for years. We *both* felt it. And you know that if you had ridden off with Robert and I had married Graham, that it would have hurt *me*. The fact that it was only some night you regret that kept you from doing it...well, that hurts me almost as much."

"The situation was...*complicated*," he said softly.

"Of course it was," she said, throwing up her hands. "I was in love with one of my brother's best friends and marrying the other. You think that hasn't torn me apart for years? That seeing you and wanting to be near you and wanting to *touch* you hasn't broken my heart and my spirit?"

His eyes went wide. "You love me."

"If you don't know that, then you are blind as well as a coward," she whispered. "Because I have never been very good at hiding it. Especially not when we were alone together."

"Meg—" he began.

She shook her head. "No. No! I know you, Simon. You're going to start reciting all these reasons why we are *wrong* and what we did was *wrong* and how we don't deserve to be happy. That *you* don't deserve it. But that is a pile of...well, it's a pile of something I'm not supposed to say as a lady. And you know it."

"I was never trying—"

"You were never *trying* at all!" She realized she was shouting. And she didn't care. She wanted to shout. She wanted to scream because she had been silent for so long.

"Do you think I *wanted* to walk away?" he snapped.

She folded her arms. "You were going to, so in this situation I suppose it doesn't matter what your intention was."

He stared at her, his mouth opening and shutting.

She shook her head. "Simon, I know you've cared for me as long as I've cared for you. But you were never willing to fight for me. And I've been fighting. I've been *fighting* since we were caught together that night in the cottage and it was clear we would be forced to marry. I knew that we could be happy, that we could be...*right*. But now I see I was a fool."

She stared at him, at his beautiful face. She saw his pain. But she also saw his hesitation. And that was what broke her, for it proved to her what she already knew.

He wasn't willing to overcome the obstacles between them. She wasn't worth it to him. And like Emma, she realized she didn't want to live a life like that. She couldn't love this man and have him incapable of allowing himself to feel the same in return.

She'd rather be alone.

She backed away, forcing a wall down between them just as he had done so many times before. "I'm leaving."

His eyes went wide. "Leaving?"

She nodded slowly. "I need time. I need to think. I'll go to James and Emma's. I just need...to not be here."

"Please, Meg," he said, moving to her. He caught her arms, but she struggled free of him even though his touch burned her with desire and love.

"*No*," she insisted. "I just need to...go."

He backed up a step, his mouth drawn down and his eyes dark with emotion. Then he nodded. "I won't stop you."

Those words were meant to give her what she wanted, but her heart sank when he said them. Because in the end, that was the problem. He *wouldn't* stop her. And that meant what she wanted was something she would never have.

She shook as she turned her back on him. She shook as she walked out of the parlor in silence. She shook as she waited for

Finley to call for a carriage. But she didn't turn back and he didn't call out for her.

In that moment, she knew it was over.

Simon paced the parlor, drink in hand, just as he had been doing for...God, he didn't know how long. Hours, for certain. The room had grown dark, then light had returned.

Meg had not.

His mind had spun all night, spun with Graham's accusations that he didn't fight, with Meg's. Their words wound together, burrowing into his soul and making him question everything he'd ever believed about himself.

He was a peacekeeper. He had been between his mother and father, he had been between those in his group. He'd spent a lifetime trying to be whatever was needed to make things...*pleasant.*

And now he was being told that it wasn't enough. Worse, he knew that it was true. But to be more, to fight, that required him to take a risk. And giving his heart, reaching for more, that had never ended well for him over the years.

"Your Grace."

He turned to find Finley in the doorway, the butler's face drawn with concern as he looked at him. And why not? The poor man kept offering him food and suggesting he take some rest, but Simon couldn't do it.

He had to find a way to deal with this and he just didn't know how.

"What is it?" he asked, his voice rough from exhaustion.

"It's me."

The butler stepped aside and James strode into the parlor. Simon froze. His best friend's face was tight and his eyes were bright with anger.

"You can leave us, Finley," Simon said softly.

The butler did so, closing the door behind him without having to be asked to do so. The moment it clicked shut, James pushed up on him, chest forward, body language nothing but aggressive. "I asked you to do one simple thing. What was it?"

"Not to hurt Meg," Simon said, and his voice cracked. "And I failed you. You want to hit me, call me out, destroy me, then do it."

"I don't want to do any of those things," James snapped. "I want to see you figure out what you need to do. What you *want* to do. And I want to see you be happy."

Simon bent his head. "I don't think I've ever been happy, James. I'm not sure I know how."

He sank into the settee and rested his head in his hands as emotions he normally controlled washed over him. He felt James sit beside him.

"I know what your life was like as a boy," James said. "Your father wasn't as overtly cruel as mine could be, he wasn't as violent as Graham's, but I know you spent your life walking a tightrope. Trying to be what everyone wanted you to be in order to keep some kind of peace. Hell, you even tried your best to keep Graham and me steady when we lost our way."

"You and he are fighters," Simon whispered. "I just don't know how to be."

"What do you want?" James asked.

"Her," Simon snapped, looking at his friend at last. He saw pity in James's face, but also understanding and both broke him. "Bloody *her*, always her, only her."

James nodded. "Then you'd better figure out how to be the man she needs, because your time is running out."

"What does that mean?"

"She was devastated when she showed up at our home yesterday," James said, his frown deepening. "I've never seen her so broken. And she..."

"She what?" Simon asked, leaning in.

"She left, Simon. She was determined that she couldn't see you again, that she couldn't know that you don't love her enough to make her a priority. She left London this morning."

Simon leapt up. "Left? Where did she go?"

"Back to Falcon's Landing," James said with a sigh. "I tried to talk her out of it, said that I would mediate between you. Emma tried to convince her too, she even invoked our unborn child in an attempt to guilt her into remaining. But Meg just kept saying that you hated yourself more than you loved her and she wouldn't be a part of it anymore."

Simon stared at his friend, the words that James was saying settling into his skin, his soul, his mind and his heart. They mixed with Meg's accusation that he was a coward, with Graham's harsh words about Simon never fighting for what he wanted. It stewed together and, without thinking, Simon tilted his head back and let out a roar that all but shook the room.

James rose slowly as Simon panted through the intense emotions that ripped him apart.

"I have to go after her," Simon gasped out at last when he could speak. "I have to follow her."

For weeks James had only looked at him with a combination of concern and contempt, but now his friend's lips turned up slightly. "It took you long enough to figure *that* out. What will you do?"

"What I should have done from the start," he said. "What I was afraid to do for all these years. I'm going to be honest. I'm going to be open. And I'm going to…to fight for what she is and what I want. And I won't take no for an answer, even if she gives it to me for ten years. I won't back away until she knows that I am just as invested in her as she is in me."

"She loves you," James said softly.

He bent his head. "I haven't deserved it before. I was so convinced that I couldn't sacrifice anyone else's needs to get what I wanted. But I'm going to fight to deserve it from now on."

"Good. That will be a start," James said, clapping him on the arm. "So when do you go?"

"I have a few things to prepare," he said, wishing he could rush headlong toward Meg right that instant and throw himself on her mercy. But he had hurt her for too long and too deeply to think that was enough atonement. He needed to prove himself to her. That would take planning.

And perhaps a few days to herself would make her more open to what he wanted to give.

"I'm going to fix this, James," Simon said, locking eyes with his friend. "First with Meg, and then with Graham."

"Worry about Meg now," James suggested. "Now what can I do to help?"

Simon thought on it a moment, then nodded as a plan began to take shape in his mind. "Well, first I need the very powerful Duke of Abernathe to send word to his servants…"

CHAPTER 19

M eg strolled through the garden behind her brother's country estate and let out a long sigh. Falcon's Landing had always been an escape for her, a pleasure. But she'd been home for five days and she felt none of those things. Instead, when she looked around her, all she saw were reminders of Simon.

There in the corner of the garden, just beside the fountain, was where she had first met him. Up on the terrace was where he had once spun her in a dance the night she came out to Society and had been so nervous she almost couldn't move. How many times had they whispered private little jokes and stories to each other at suppers at the table in the dining room?

And then there was her room. Once a sanctuary, all she could think of now when she laid her head on her pillows was that this was the place where Simon had come and claimed her innocence after they'd been forced to announce their engagement.

Every place she looked was him. Was *them*.

And it was so desperately unfair since she knew that "them" was a lie she'd told herself. Simon would never allow a "them" to exist. Not really.

In the end, she supposed she'd have to just sequester herself away. Perhaps James and Emma would allow her to build some kind of little cottage on the edge of the property, a place that would hold no memories of Simon. A place where he had never touched her.

God knew he'd probably be just as happy to be estranged. Then she wouldn't be a constant reminder of all he had betrayed and lost.

"Your Grace?"

She turned to find Grimble coming down the path toward her. She wrinkled her brow, for the very proper butler was hardly ever seen outside the confines of the house.

"Is there something I can do for you, Grimble?" she asked, clearing her mind of all her maudlin thoughts as best she could.

"There is a bit of a problem that I fear requires addressing," the butler said, stopping before her and shifting with discomfort. "A household issue."

Meg nodded slowly. "I see. Well, what is it?"

"You know that caretaker cottage a few miles down the road on the property?"

Meg froze at the mention of the caretaker cottage. That was probably why Grimble was shifting so furiously now. Everyone knew what had transpired there between her and Simon. Well, they thought they knew, anyway.

"Yes, I think you know I know the spot," Meg managed to croak out and Grimble blushed slightly. "What is it?"

"Well, Toby was going out to market earlier today and happened to take the long path through the estate. He noticed that some damage had been done to the cottage, and he feared some items inside might be missing."

Meg folded her arms. "Grimble, I appreciate the importance of the issue, but why are you addressing this to me? It seems like something the estate staff could handle quite well on their own. Have them begin to repair the damage and take an inventory. Then write to Abernathe to let him know of the situation."

Grimble cleared his throat. "Yes. Of course. I shall do that, but you see, you were the last person to be inside the cottage, Your

Grace. And since there may be items missing, we thought it would be best if *you* could go and make some kind of list of anything you notice amiss."

Meg shook her head. "I-I may have been there recently, but I couldn't—"

She stopped herself. It was amazing how physical her reaction to this situation was. The very idea of going to the caretaker cottage again made anxious tingles run through her body. To go back there, to face that place…

Grimble was staring at her. "I do not want to cause you discomfort, Your Grace, of course. I only thought you might be able to help."

Meg sighed. "No, you aren't…it—it isn't your fault, Grimble. And you are right, as the last person on the estate who was at the cottage, I might be the best judge of what is to be found there." She stared off through the garden for a moment, trying to calm herself as she considered her options. "I could use a ride anyway. I'll go past the cottage and have a look."

Grimble almost sagged with relief. "Thank you, Your Grace. That would be most appreciated."

She shook her head. "I'll go change. Will you ask that Star be saddled for me?"

"Yes, Your Grace," Grimble said, falling into step beside her. "And I'll have a picnic lunch prepared for you, as well."

Meg did her best not to let out a deep sigh. Her broken heart must be very obvious, indeed, to have Grimble so forcefully pushing her to make half a day of her excursion. But perhaps he was right that it would do her some good to get away. She'd look in on the cottage, make her observations and then take a long ride.

"Very good," she said as they entered the house and she headed for the stairs. "I'll be down shortly."

She moved to her chamber and rang for Fran to help her into her habit. It had been a long time since she rode and Star was her favorite mount, but despite all that, she didn't look forward to it.

Going back to the caretaker cottage felt like returning to a scene of a crime. And right now she wasn't ready to face that, or all the feelings that still boiled inside of her that would likely never be resolved.

S imon saw the rider coming long before she arrived. He caught his breath and lifted his spyglass to his eye as he leaned against the window. Meg wore a dark blue riding habit and a jaunty hat, but when he caught a glimpse of her face, his heart sank. She looked utterly miserable.

And it was going to take a lion's share of work to fix that.

He put the glass away and looked around. He had been in Abernathe for two days. Two days of hard work had put the caretaker cottage into good shape, ready for Meg and all his plans for her.

If she would stay, that was. If he had not done so much damage that she would turn away from any offer he made, not trusting him.

In the past, such a possibility would have perhaps put him off. But not today. Not with Meg. With Meg, he had to fight. It was what she needed, what she deserved. And perhaps for the first time in his life, it was what he wanted to do.

He wanted to earn her.

He heard her pulling up to the cottage. She said soft words to her mare. It was time.

He drew in a long breath, and walked to the door and outside to greet her.

She was staring up at the cottage but when he exited the house, that expression changed. For a brief moment he saw pure joy when she looked at him, love, desire, pleasure. But then those were wiped away. Pain slashed across her face and she brought a wall down between them that he knew he was entirely responsible for.

But he'd seen the joy. He knew there was a chance for them.

"Simon," she breathed, taking a long step back. "I—what are you —how—?"

He moved toward her a step, careful not to crowd her but wanting, *needing*, to be closer. "I apologize for the subterfuge."

Her lips parted and she stared at the cottage again. "There was *never* any damage to the house, was there? Nothing missing?"

He shook his head. "No. I've been here for some time, arranging things, readying them. James wrote ahead to Grimble to encourage him to act as I asked him to. So don't blame him for—"

"Lying?" she interrupted, folding her arms.

He nodded. "Lying is correct, I suppose."

"And why go to such lengths?" she asked, her voice going softer. "Why not just ride up to the house and demand I see you? As my husband, you have that right."

He wrinkled his brow. "Do you think that is my personality, Meg? To make demands on you? To force you to feel or do something you don't wish to do?"

"Well, you created an elaborate lie to make me do something I don't wish to do," she retorted.

"See me?"

Her bottom lip trembled slightly and then she shook her head. "I will be honest where you will not. I-I am happy to see you. I am always happy to see you. But I'm also...also...angry. And hurt. And I don't want to go around and around in circles with you anymore. We've played that game far too long."

"It's not a game," he whispered.

She shook her head slowly. "Why are you here, Simon? Why follow me when you've made your intentions so very clear over the past month?"

He wanted so much to bend his head, to pull away from her anger. But he wouldn't. Not ever again. With much difficulty, he moved toward her another step and reached for her hand. As he took it, she trembled, but she didn't back away.

"I came here because I know I have made a mess of everything, Meg. You said I didn't fight. Actually, so did Graham...so did James. And you are all correct. My nature is to do something else entirely.

But when you left London, when it was clear you were surrendering in the battle for our future, I realized that losing you would be the worst thing to ever happen to me. I know I'm late, I know I'm maybe too late. But I've come here to fight, Meg. Fight for you."

Her lips parted, and he could see how much those words meant to her. But she didn't fall into his arms. She didn't launch into a soliloquy of her love for him. Instead she gently removed her hand from his.

"I don't know, Simon. I just don't know," she whispered.

He nodded. "And that's fine. I know for both of us. I don't ask you to forgive me right away. I don't ask you to make me promises. But I'm asking you to let me try. Will you do that?"

She shifted her weight, but her gaze never left his. She was struggling with what he requested, afraid she would be hurt again. In that moment, she was so entirely beautiful that he couldn't resist. He stepped in, closing the space between them.

He tucked a finger beneath her chin and tilted her mouth toward his. He brushed his lips against hers, reveling in the kiss he had been longing for since the day she walked out of the parlor. She opened to him with a little sigh and he gently took what she offered, working hard not to get swept away by passion because he needed to be levelheaded for his plans.

At last, he drew back, seeing her confusion and her need and her pain still merged together in her tortured expression.

"Please, Meg, let me try to be the man I should have been from the beginning."

She let out a long sigh and then she nodded. "Very well."

"Excellent!" he said, backing away from her with great difficulty and clapping his hands together. "Then remove that picnic bag from Star's saddle and I'll bind her to a post for the servants to collect her."

Meg stared at him. "How do you know there's a picnic bundle and that—" She cut herself off with a shake of her head. "Oh, I see. You've arranged *everything*."

"I've tried." He motioned her toward the horse. "Go on then."

She actually smiled as she did as she was told. When she removed the saddlebag, she grunted. "Good Lord, there's enough in here for days."

"I hope so," he said, guiding the horse to a post near the cottage and securing her there. "That was what I asked for."

She met his eyes briefly. "How long am I to stay out here with you?"

"As long as you agree to," he said with a shrug. "As long as you don't run out of clothing, which will be delivered when they come to take the horse."

"How many servants are in on your scheme?" she asked, shaking her head.

He grinned. "Not many. Grimble, obviously, and Fran. Plus whomever they involved. But this isn't about anyone else but us."

She turned her face away and he frowned. She wasn't ready to believe him yet. And that was fine. He was ready to fight now. He was actually looking forward to it. It was the first thing that had felt right in his life for years.

He slung the saddlebag over his shoulder and reached for her hand. She focused on his outstretched fingers for a moment, and he could see her mind turning. But at last she took them. He squeezed gently and then guided her out onto the path and away from the cottage into the same woods they had roamed the afternoon both their lives had changed.

But that day wasn't the only thing he wanted Meg to remember. They had shared many a day in these woods. Many a memory that he hoped would guide her back to him.

She was silent for a while as they walked, then she let out a breath like she'd been holding it for a while. "What do you want me to do?"

He stopped in the path and turned toward her. "Nothing. You've been doing everything for a long time. Let *me* do something now. Just…be open. That's all I have to ask."

Her lower lip trembled. "Why now?"

"I would tell you that it's because I love you. That it's because I've loved you for a decade. That it's because the thought of losing you actually cuts away a piece of my heart."

Tears swelled in her eyes, and he wanted so desperately to wipe them away or make some kind of joke to diminish their power, but he didn't. It was time to show them. Time to show her everything that was in his heart, uncomfortable or not. Withholding himself from her had nearly made him lose her. Now he had to give her everything.

"But I'm not going to tell you that," he continued. "Because right now my words are meaningless without something more behind them. So I'm going to show you how I feel, Meg. And I only hope that it's going to be enough."

CHAPTER 20

S imon sat on the ground, laying out food and drinks across the blanket that had been tucked into the saddlebag. He was very focused on the act, which gave her time to observe him.

When she'd ridden up to the cottage and he'd stepped out to greet her, every part of her heart and soul had screamed at her to launch herself into his arms.

But she hadn't. And he hadn't asked her to do so. He'd only asked for her open mind, and she was trying to give it. It was almost impossible when he did things like quietly and calmly declare his love for her, but then deny that she should decide her future only on his words.

It would be easy to do that, for those words were what she'd wanted to hear for so many years.

"Are you certain you don't need help?" she asked, shifting on her feet as he set a fallen wine goblet upright for the third time.

"No, I can manage this," he said, and smiled in triumph as the glass stayed in place at last. "Come join me."

She laughed as she did so and settled onto the blanket. The spread was lovely, with cold chicken, fresh bread and enough cheese to satisfy even her. He prepared a plate for her and handed it over, along with a glass of wine, then made a plate for himself.

She smiled at him. "You know what this reminds me of?"

His eyes lit up. "That picnic we all went on when you were, what...sixteen?"

She nodded. "James was so lost when he first inherited. I think it was the first time he laughed when he was duke."

"He and Graham went to fish, didn't they?" Simon asked.

She shivered as she thought of that long ago day. "And you and I were left alone."

His own smile fell. "It was the first time we were alone since your engagement. I was trying to maintain a distance, but all I wanted to do was kiss you," he whispered.

She shrugged. "I *wanted* you to kiss me, but I knew you wouldn't."

"I should have," he said, scooting a little closer. Close enough that she felt the warmth of his skin, the brush of his breath against her cheek. "I should have thrown caution to the wind and kissed you right then and there. I should have told Graham and James that I wanted to marry you. I should have told *you*."

"Why didn't you?" she whispered, looking up at him, drawn in by all the passion she knew was between them but knowing that would never be enough to sustain their happiness. That had been proven already.

He reached out and dragged his fingertips across her jawline, letting his thumb trace her lower lip gently. "Honor," he whispered.

She frowned. There was that word again. Honor had been the foundation of all the walls he put between them.

He continued, "I would have told you then that it was honor that stopped me. But that wasn't it. Not really."

Her eyes went wide at that admission. "What was it?"

"Fear," he admitted, and it was clear how difficult that word was to say. She saw it in the darkening of his cheeks, in the way his eyes darted away. "It's no excuse, but I spent my life trying to fit a mold, trying to please unpleasant parents. If I edged the wrong way, everything I wanted was withheld."

She and Emma had discussed this, that Simon had not been raised to fight, but to please. And she understood his desire to make things right rather than to ask for what he wanted. "I do understand. I've seen the way your mother treats you even now. It wasn't right to make you dance for your reward. Not when the reward was love."

He cocked his head. "I never knew love until I met my friends. That was brotherhood and acceptance. And I was afraid to lose it. And honestly…" He trailed off and then shook his head. "Bloody hell, this is difficult to say."

She took his hands and squeezed gently. "Just say it."

He nodded. "What if I risked it, Meg? What if I had leaned in and kissed you and told you everything in my heart? And then you'd… hated me for it. And *they'd* hated me for it. I was terrified I'd lose everything that I held dear and end up alone again."

She flinched. "So you didn't try."

"No," he said with a sigh. "I didn't try. It was cowardly of me."

She watched him carefully, his drawn face, his torn expression. She had always loved Simon for his ability to make light of difficult situations. For the way he acted as peacemaker when it was needed. In truth, that made them very alike.

So alike that neither of them had tried for more, even when they both desperately wanted it. Wanted each other.

She pushed to her feet and smiled down at him. "Come."

He wrinkled his brow. "You don't want to eat?"

"After."

"After what?" he asked, his tone wary as he got to his feet.

She laughed. "It is one of the last warm days in the fall and that lake will soon be too cold to swim in. I always wanted to do it, but was discouraged once I was a young woman. Not appropriate, they said."

His eyes went wide. "You want to swim in the lake with me."

She nodded, then turned her back to him. "Unfasten me, will you?"

There was a beat of hesitation, then she felt his hands sliding across her shoulders, to the buttons along the back of her habit. When he'd loosened her, she shed it, along with the plain shift dress beneath, leaving her in only her chemise. When she turned, he'd already stripped out of his shirt and unfastened his trousers, which now slung low on defined hips.

He smiled at her. "Having second thoughts?"

She thought on that question. It felt like it contained more power to it than just a teasing question about going into the lake. She held out her hand and shook her head. "No."

He laughed as he kicked out of his trousers and she caught her breath at the sight of him, naked. It had been several days since the last time she saw him like this. Made love to him. Now all she could do was stare and marvel at his physical perfection. All that muscle, all that taut skin stretching across it. God, he was perfect.

When she bit her lip, his cock hardened and she jerked her gaze to his face to find him staring at her expectantly. "Swim or something else?" he asked, teasing and seductive all at once.

She slipped her chemise off so she was as naked as he was, and reveled in the way his pupils dilated with need. Her breath short, she moved closer and brushed her lips against his neck. "Both."

He chuckled low in his throat, then surprised her by sweeping her into his arms and carrying her into the water. He tossed her in and she squealed in pleasure as she hit the cool water and submerged. When she paddled to the surface, he was waiting for her, already wet, his hair slicked back from where he'd dunked himself.

She splashed him as she laughed and he dove in her direction. She backstroked away just as swiftly, kicking as she laughed in a way she hadn't allowed herself to do for years.

"Little minx," he sputtered as she hit him square in the face with a wave of water. He lunged and caught her ankle, dragging her toward him.

She wrapped her arms around his neck as he flattened her to his chest, and suddenly her laughter faded. So did his. They bobbed together, her wet breasts pressing against his chest, his cock making itself known in the space between their bodies.

"I missed you," he whispered.

She smiled. "I've been here all along."

He shook his head. "But I haven't. I admit that. All those years, we became such good friends, and I loved that. But I also pushed you further and further away because I knew you'd be taken from me. It became a habit to distance myself."

"To protect yourself," she suggested softly.

"Yes, I suppose so. And since we wed, I've done it even more. Out of some sense of guilt and disappointment in myself. But also out of fear that you would stop loving me. That I would let you down if you got too close. And I've missed my best friend."

"Graham?" she murmured, her heart throbbing at all these things he said and admitted.

He cupped her chin. "My best friend was always you."

He kissed her, his wet lips claiming hers, his tongue taking deeply and completely. She shuddered against him, her nails digging into his broad shoulders as he caught her legs and wrapped them around his waist in the water.

"And now I want to do things to you that are not something friends do," he murmured, his voice rough.

She shifted and felt his cock pressed at her entrance. "Like this?" she asked as she slid lower and took him inside of her on smooth thrust.

He rested his forehead on hers. "Oh yes, most definitely that."

Their panting breaths merged as they rocked their hips together. The slick slide of him, the water sloshing around them, the way his hips rubbed against her pelvis, stimulating her clitoris, it was all perfect. She lifted into him, kissing him deeply as the pleasure built and built and finally she spasmed out her pleasure.

He followed swiftly after, groaning out her name as he pumped his release deep inside of her. He kept her in his arms, their bodies intertwined as he carried her through the water, still kissing. Her legs were still locked around him as he exited the lake.

He set her on the blanket carefully and then moved the food so none would spill before he took a place beside her, laying on his back, both still utterly naked. The afternoon sun warmed her wet flesh as she stared up at him.

"I can only imagine the reaction if we'd done *that* at that picnic all those years ago." She said with a laugh.

He didn't join her in her laughter. "Life certainly would have been very different if I'd taken that chance." He glanced at the water. "Well, perhaps not *that* one. But the chance to say something then."

She sat up and kissed him. "Come on, I'm hungry. Let's eat, yes?"

He nodded and they dove into the food before them, but she could see he was still troubled by all the talk about the past. And in truth, so was she. For there was more to discuss before they could move on to what the future held for them.

Meg was smiling as she and Simon approached the caretaker cottage together hours after their passionate encounter in the lake. He smiled, too, though he knew he had a long way to go still to earn Meg back. He'd made headway, of course. She had opened herself to him, allowed him in as they talked as well as when they made love, but he knew her hesitance remained.

He opened the door and they were met with warmth and delicious scents. The servants had done as he'd asked—a fire now burned in the hearth and a fresh basket of food was set on the table. She laughed as she looked at him. "Did you hire sprites to do these things and then disappear?"

He shrugged. "If I told you all my secrets, I would no longer be mysterious and you'd bore of me. Now, why don't you go into the bedroom? If my sprites have done as they were asked, then you should have a bath waiting for you."

Her eyes went wide. "You arranged for a bath for me?"

He nodded. "I didn't expect we'd take a dunk in the lake together, but I thought it might be nice after a day out and about in the woods."

She eased up closer, staring up at him with those dark eyes he was forever lost in. "And will you be joining me, Your Grace?"

He swallowed hard. "There is nothing I'd like more, but I have a few things to prepare."

She held her gaze on him a long moment and he could see her mind turning. She was judging him, analyzing his every move. He couldn't help but wonder what decisions she was coming to.

"Very well," she said at last, then lifted to her tiptoes to kiss him and slipped into the bedroom.

When the door was closed, he took a long breath. Just being near Meg set him on his head. Made him dizzy. She always had. It seemed she always would. And today had repaired some of the damage he'd caused between them. They had been friends today, as well as lovers. When they talked it wasn't just about their marriage or their past, it had been easy and comfortable.

All that gave him hope, but not enough. There was more work to do to prove that he wouldn't fall back into old habits, that he wouldn't push her away out of some sense of fear or honor or self-punishment.

He moved about the room, lighting candles and lamps, stoking the fire, and then he carefully prepared their food for the night. When it was all finished, he moved to the bedroom door and knocked gently.

"Come in," she called out.

He stepped inside and caught his breath. The fire burned bright in this room too and Meg had lit the candles, as well. The big tub was pulled right in front of the fire and the light spilled over her. She had pulled her damp hair up into a loose bun on top of her head, and her long neck and high cheekbones were accentuated beautifully.

The water was cloudy from soap, but he still caught glimpses of pink flesh that drove him mad. "You do tempt a man," he murmured as he sank down on his knees beside the tub, resting his arms on the edge.

She smiled, but there was fire in her eyes. That fire he'd always been drawn to like a moth. "Tempt you enough to join me?" she whispered, leaning forward. The tops of her breasts bobbed out of the water, giving him a peekaboo glimpse of hard nipples, and he groaned.

"Next time," he promised. "Next time I will join you."

She smiled and leaned up, dampening his shirt as she kissed him. "If you say so." She sighed and leaned back. "This was wonderful, thank you."

"You deserved it," he said softly, rolling up his sleeves as he spoke. "You deserve so much more than I've given."

Her expression softened, even as he dipped his hand beneath the water and stroked his fingers back and forth over her knee.

"Simon, you judge yourself so harshly. Have there been mistakes made? Yes. But that is being human. To expect you'd go through life without ever making the wrong move is to hold yourself to a high standard that is unattainable."

He met her stare, stilling his fingers in their movement. "But I've hurt you."

She nodded. "You have. But I've never thought you did it with malice or intent or forethought."

"It doesn't matter," he said, his heart hurting.

"Yes, it does," she whispered. "If I thought you'd meant to hurt me or taken pleasure in that act, I would have asked you to leave instead of joining you today. I grew up with a man who enjoyed hurting those around him, who did things on purpose to break us down. Whatever you've done, I know you are not that man."

His eyes fluttered shut and he let out a long breath as pain overwhelmed him. "You overcame just as much as I did from your childhood, but you are so much better, Meg. So much stronger."

She moved forward again, cupping his cheeks gently. "I had James as my support," she reminded him. "You were alone until you met Graham and James when you were, what, thirteen? And even then, it wasn't as if you always had them at your side. You are exactly who you are, Simon. I wouldn't want any other man, any other way."

He met her eyes, he saw the truth in her words, and the love he felt for her washed over him. He leaned in and kissed her, drawing her almost out of the tub as he crushed her against him and reveled in her warmth and her acceptance, things he had shied away from since their marriage because, in truth, he hadn't believed he deserved them. Or that they were real. Or that they could last.

Now he was beginning to believe. To see the future she had described so many times. The one he had nearly destroyed out of fear and distrust that love could be true.

He drew away, shaking from the power of his emotions. "I'm sorry."

She laughed as she stood up, a goddess clad only in rivulets of streaming water. "Never apologize for kissing your wife thoroughly, Simon."

He grabbed for one of the thick towels the servants had brought to the cottage earlier in the day. She wrapped herself in it, drying off slowly as she smiled at him, well-aware of the show she was performing. And every part of his body was on high alert as she did so.

Somehow, though, he resisted her temptations and took the robe that lay across the bed. "Your Grace."

She shrugged into it, and followed him into the main room of the cottage. He offered her a seat at the table and she stared down at the place he'd set for her. When she smiled, he tilted his head. "What?"

She laughed as she switched the knives and forks around. "You set it all backward."

He grinned. "How am I to know?"

"You don't pay attention when you sit down to eat?" she giggled.

He shrugged. "It seems I don't. Perhaps I am too caught up in the company I keep to know which side is for knives and which for forks."

"Of course. That must be it."

He set food on her plate and his own, then sat down across from her. The table was so small that it was an intimate setting, and for a while they ate in companionable silence.

But as time ticked by, Simon knew he couldn't put off the inevitable for long. At last, he set his napkin on the table and met her gaze.

"I've avoided your questions and your concerns these past few weeks," he said. "And tonight I want to address them. So if you have something you want to ask, if you have something you need to know...I'm here to answer."

She caught her breath, a sharp intake of air that told him she was surprised by his openness. She set her own napkin away and leaned back in her chair. "You are truly dedicated to this, aren't you?" she whispered.

He nodded. "Yes, I am. The moment James told me you'd left, I realized that was like my own heart being torn from my chest. I was late in recognizing that losing you would be the closest thing to death, but I see it now and I will do anything to keep it from happening."

She pressed her lips together for a moment. "Very well, then I open the floor to the same openness from my end. If you have any questions for me, I shall answer them with the same spirit of honesty that you have given."

He drew back, for he hadn't considered that as an option. He realized he did, indeed, have questions for Meg. But he wanted to clear her mind before he addressed his own. "You first."

She ducked her head and a dark blush colored her cheeks. The unexpected reaction surprised him.

"What is it?"

"I'm trying to find a way to phrase my question," she admitted. "Er, the morning James and Graham found us here, the morning everything…changed, I overheard you and my brother talking."

Simon thought back to that morning that felt like a lifetime ago. "Go on."

"He said that you…you and Roseford had…"

She trailed off, her cheeks going even darker, and Simon flinched as he recalled his conversation with James that morning. He cleared his throat. "You heard James say that Roseford and I had shared women in the past. And that I whored my way through London for years."

"Yes," she whispered. "In fact, I have sometimes wondered if that was part of your hesitation about…*us*. Although I have very much enjoyed the education you've given me since our engagement, I know I am an innocent when it comes to pleasures of the flesh. Perhaps I am not enough for you."

His eyes went wide at that thought. "No!" he cried. "No, Meg, that isn't it at all." He pushed to his feet and paced away, running a hand through his hair. He had no idea how to explain what he'd done to her. How to make her understand. In the end, he settled on the truth. "I sowed my wild oats like many a young man," he said. "Pleasure is…well, pleasure helps one forget pain, even if only for a moment."

She nodded as if she understood that, and perhaps she did, considering their volatile relationship these last few weeks and the passions they had explored together. "And the sharing part?"

Simon swallowed. "After you were engaged to Graham, I was lost. Yes, I spiraled into debauchery for a while, hoping that a woman or five women or ten would make me forget the only one I truly wanted. Roseford and I shared a woman a few times, and I won't deny that it was pleasurable. But it was empty. No one was you. And you were all I wanted. In truth, in the last few years I have hardly touched another woman. I had no stomach for it anymore."

Her eyes were wide when he dared to look at her again. "So... wait, are you saying you were trying to..."

"Forget that it was you I wanted," he answered with a nod. "Yes."

Her expression softened. "And you don't want that sort of thing now?"

He shook his head. "All I want is you and the thought of some other man touching you, even if I were in the room with you helping you find pleasure, makes me want to punch the wall."

Relief flooded her features. "I'm so glad. The idea I wouldn't be enough for you—"

"Meg, I want to make it clear," he said. "Whether you accept me back into your life as your husband again or not. Whatever happens to us in the future, I will *never* touch another woman again as long as I live. You are and always have been, more than enough for me."

She blinked. "You would not touch another woman, even I refused you?"

"I recognize it doesn't seem like I've taken our vows very seriously, but I do. *You* are my wife and my love and I will never betray you."

"Thank you," she whispered, her voice thick with tears and emotions. She rose and moved closer to him. "And now I think it's your turn to ask me a question."

He hesitated for a long moment, and then he said, "You wept the night you and Graham announced the date for your wedding. And you've told me many times that you didn't want to marry him. We've discussed why *I* never intervened, but why—" He cut himself off, not wanting to make an accusation toward her.

She leaned closer. "Why?" she encouraged.

He sucked in a deep breath and met her eyes. "Why didn't you stop it? If you didn't want to marry Graham, why didn't you tell James no?"

CHAPTER 21

Meg caught her breath at the direct question. Simon didn't ask it with malice or accusation in his tone, but he also didn't move his gaze from hers. And she knew why. He had taken the blame all this time for the situation they found themselves in.

The moment had finally come for her to accept her own share.

"James went through so much at the hands of our father," she began with a shake of her head.

"You *both* did."

She smiled at his gentle defense of her. "Yes, but I didn't have the weight of inheritance on my shoulders like my brother did. The weight of what he thought would be failure. It was hard for him to carry."

Simon nodded. "I remember those dark days."

"When James announced that I would marry Graham, he was so happy. He thought he was doing the right thing, that he'd made his first act as duke the best one possible. I had no idea how to respond. My ears were ringing, my hands were shaking. I looked at you across the room, because I thought perhaps you liked me as much as I did you."

His face fell. "And I offered no resistance, thanks to my own shock about what was happening."

Pain flooded her at the memory, but she understood so much more now. About him. About herself. "I was very young, you know. I had no experience, I thought perhaps I had misread the situation. That you truly only did want to be a friend to me. If that were true, there would be no point in shattering James's hopes. So I convinced myself that you didn't want me and that I could get over wanting you."

"But you didn't," he said softly.

"No," she agreed. "I never did, no matter how I tried. And I *never* loved Graham, no matter how much I wished I could. Perhaps I should have said something as the years stretched out. There were times I thought I might. But it felt more and more impossible to do that as Society became more invested in my nuptials with Graham. The scandal if I broke it off—"

"Yes, I understand," he said, letting out a long sigh of regret. "It kept me silent, as well."

She shook her head slowly. "In a way, Simon, we are so alike. Both wanting to please those around us, never wanting to disappoint or hurt them. And in the end, it made both of us cowards. It made *both* of us turn away from the future we wanted."

"I suppose it did. For a while. But now we're here. And I hope that we can overcome our mistakes of the past. I want to."

She believed him. It was impossible not to when he was so sincere and so honest about their past. But she still wasn't quite ready to give in to what he offered. To give the heart that he had crushed a few days before.

He examined her closely. "You're still not certain. Does that mean you have another question for *me*?"

"I-I do." She felt the lump in her throat, the pain that spread through her as she stared at this man, her husband, her love. There was only one more thing that she carried with her now. But it was the biggest heartache of her life. The one fact that would keep her from fully trusting this man. "Would you have truly left with Roseford? Would you have walked away and let me marry another?"

His face twitched, pain slashing across it. The moment seemed to stretch out forever, an eternity of struggle for them both as he searched for whatever words he was going to say. "Why do you think I followed you that afternoon when we were trapped together?"

She shrugged. "We were friends and you saw me struggling. You—"

"No," he interrupted.

She blinked at the forcefulness of his tone. "No?"

"No," he said, softer this time. "I knew I shouldn't, Meg. I knew I should get James or Graham to go after you. I followed you because I...I knew in some part of me that doing so would seal my fate. I told Roseford I wanted to leave, I told myself I would step aside as I always had and allow your future to unfold without me. But I followed you here, Meg. And I *let* us get caught in a storm."

"What do you mean?" she whispered.

"I was following you for an hour before I stopped you. Don't you think I noticed the gathering clouds? Don't you think I knew exactly what might happen if I didn't steer you home before they opened up a torrent?" He paced a moment. "Once we were trapped, I still had options that would keep the scandal at a minimum. But I stayed in this cottage with you. And I kissed you at last. And I did all of it so the decision would be removed from my hands. So I could take you from Graham without having to be man enough to admit it was what I wanted all along."

His face was bright with emotion now, his blue eyes stormy and filled with many things, not one of which was regret.

"You're saying you manipulated what happened?"

"Perhaps I didn't allow myself to know that at the time, but... yes," he whispered. "The fact is, Meg, I can say that I wouldn't have walked away, because I didn't. I *didn't* walk away. And I know that it is hard to believe based on my past, based on what I've done before and since we wed, but I'm telling you right now I will *never* walk away again. I will *never* give you another reason to believe *you* must. I will fight for you, Meg. From this day until the day I draw my last breath. I will fight for you because you are all I have ever wanted, all I have ever needed and all I shall ever desire."

She stared at him, stunned both by his words and the strength with which he said them. For the first time in years, he looked at her with clear eyes, with his intentions written across his handsome face, with all his love out in the open for her to see and embrace and adore.

And in that moment, it was enough. More than enough. It was everything.

She moved toward him, tears beginning to sting her eyes, and caught his hands. "I love you, Simon. I love you."

He didn't answer her with words, but drew her against him, dropping his mouth to hers for a kiss. For the first time, there was no desperation to the kiss. No feeling that it might be their last. There was only tenderness, desire and love. She melted against him, hardly noticing as he steered her into the bedroom, untying her robe as they stumbled together.

He stripped the fabric away and tossed it aside. When his hands trembled, she smiled. "It isn't as if you haven't seen me like this before."

He nodded. "I have. But until this moment, I've never fully accepted that you were mine."

She caught her breath. "Well, I *am* yours. And *you* are mine."

"Forever," he whispered, that word a vow to her that meant more than any they had said in the chapel. Tonight it was a surrender, a gift of faith, a promise of a future.

And she reached for him, tangling her arms around his neck as she lifted her mouth to his and returned that promise with her body. With her everything.

He helped her onto the bed and quickly stripped out of his clothing. She opened her arms to him as he joined her on the bed, his heated gaze branding her in a way it never had before. This was full surrender and she bathed in the glow of it.

His mouth came down on her throat, and he began to slowly kiss and caress his way along the length of her body. She gasped as he pleasured her tight nipples, sucking hard and laving each with his tongue until her vision blurred and wet heat soaked the inside of her thighs.

Then he dragged his mouth lower, licking her stomach, her hip, and finally he settled between her legs, opening her wide so that he could lavish her sex with long strokes of his tongue. She rose up against him, thrashing her head against the pillows as pleasure arced from and spread through every nerve in her body. She fisted the coverlet, gasping out his name as she reached for release.

He smiled up her body and then she felt his fingers slide inside her slick sheath. He curled them gently, finding some spot inside of her that sang in tune to his touch. He flicked her clitoris with his tongue and her entire body erupted with pleasure unlike anything she'd ever known.

She jolted against him, her cries uncontrollable, her body shaking almost off the bed with the force of her orgasm. He stroked her through it, pressing pleasure right to the edge of pain as she begged him for more and begged him to stop all in one ragged breath.

At last, her body relaxed, the tremors softening, and only then did he slide back up her body, opening her legs with his thighs and thrusting into her as his mouth crushed hers. She tasted her own essence on his tongue, the sweet flavor of her release, and it awakened pleasure in her all the more.

His thrusts were heavy and hard and she lifted into every one of them, reveling in the joining of their bodies, the union that could be defined or seen by no one but themselves. She felt his body tensing as he neared release, and ground her hips against him to hasten him to pleasure.

Of course, it brought her back to the edge to do so, and as her orgasm tore through her again, he gasped out her name and together they found release. When it was over, he collapsed over her, taking great breaths as she smoothed her hands over his shoulders, his back. The weight of him was everything she'd ever wanted and when he rolled away from her, she whimpered her dissatisfaction.

He chuckled. "I only don't want to crush you."

She curled into his side, wrapping her arm around him as she tucked her head into his shoulder. "It would be the way I'd choose to go."

He shook his head as he pressed a kiss to her temple. "No, you must stay forever. I have too much planned for us, for our future. That is, if you'll allow it."

She glanced up at him, surprised that his expression was actually still taut with worry. She cupped his chin and whispered, "Have I not made myself clear? I love you, Simon. And I see what lengths you've gone to to make it clear that you love me. That you chose me. I love you and my future is bound to yours, just as it always has been. But it's a future we haven't discussed much as we've worked through the tangled mess of our past."

"You want to know what our future holds?" he asked.

She nodded. "I do."

"We return to London," he said. "And we live our life. I never again hide that I love you and that I am proud to be your husband."

She shut her eyes, swelling with joy at that statement. "And what of Graham? Or those who would judge us for how we got to this place?"

He sighed. "I can't pretend that I haven't betrayed Graham. I did, and I must live with the consequences. But my life with you has nothing to do with that. One day he may not be so angry; one day he may be able to forgive me. But if that day never comes..." He shrugged. "So be it. I love you. And I am not sorry that you're mine."

She rolled over, covering his body with hers, feeling his muscles tighten as his arms came around her. She stared down into his face, all the joy and hope she hadn't allowed herself to feel washing over her.

"I will be yours forever, Simon," she whispered, laughing as he positioned her differently and slid his hard cock back into her body. "And I can't wait to see our future unfold."

"Neither can I," he promised as he took her once more.

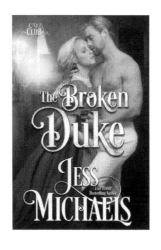

October 1810

Graham Everly, Duke of Northfield, sat in the corner of a dingy tavern, a mug of ale souring in his fist. He'd been drinking, but he wasn't drunk. Yet. He wanted to remedy that fact as quickly as possible.

But before he could take another sip, two men moved through the crowd and steered toward him. Ewan Hoffstead, Duke of Donburrow, and his cousin Matthew Cornwallis, Duke of Tyndale, both carried their own drinks, and they exchanged a not-so-subtle look before they retook their seats at his table. Graham sighed, for he was hoping the two had left already. It seemed they had not.

But then, neither of them had left his side very often in the past two months. He'd tried to avoid them, as he'd been avoiding all his friends since "the incident", as he liked to call it. But Ewan and Tyndale were relentless.

As if to demonstrate that point, Ewan dug into his overcoat pocket and drew out a small notebook and stubby charcoal pencil. He scribbled for a moment as Graham watched him. Ewan had been mute since birth, and writing was his main form of communication to friends and family.

He pushed the notebook over and Graham read the neat, even line of words written there. *"Don't sit here all night. Don't drink yourself stupid."*

Graham shoved the notebook back and glared at him. "Thanks, mate. You know, it's possible drinking won't make me stupid. I may just be stupid without the help."

Ewan shook his head with a flash of a grin at the self-deprecation, but there was no mistaking the concern in his dark eyes.

Tyndale seemed no less worried as he leaned in and said, "Come on, you can't deny it even if you make light of it. You've been stalking London pubs for two months, avoiding everyone who loves you. I recognize the signs, you know."

Graham flinched. If anyone would, Tyndale did. After all, the woman he'd loved had died years ago, devastating Tyndale down to his core. A fact which made Graham's problems seem very small. But he really didn't want to discuss this topic. It was exactly why he'd been avoiding his entire group of friends all this time. He didn't want to commiserate. He wanted to forget.

"I'm with you two, aren't I?" he growled, once again making light of the subject he could see the other two were determined to address.

Ewan wrote something and shoved it over. *"Well, we don't love you."*

Despite himself, Graham began to laugh and Matthew joined in. For a moment, his troubles faded, but then they settled back on his shoulders. And this time it didn't seem like he could avoid the topic as easily as he had been able to before.

"Look," he said, pushing his drink aside. "I know I should get over this. But Crestwood was one of my best friends and he betrayed me with what happened with Margaret."

Matthew's expression softened. "She was your fiancée, Northfield. And it's a complicated situation given their feelings for each other, but no matter the circumstances, Simon shouldn't have...*taken* her like he did. It *was* wrong."

"No one begrudges you the pain you must feel," Ewan added. *"We only worry about how you choose to express it."*

Graham stared at the words on Ewan's notebook and sighed. He had been engaged to Margaret Rylon, the sister of another of their group, for seven long years. He hadn't ever loved her, even though he'd tried desperately to make that feeling come into his heart.

But the idea that Simon would betray him...Simon, who had been like his brother since they were thirteen...well, that kept him up at night. "It isn't about her, you know."

Matthew nodded and there was that flicker of sadness in his expression again. "I know."

"We need to get you back into the world," Ewan wrote, then clapped Graham on the shoulder. *"It's time, don't you think?"*

Graham shifted. They were right, of course. He'd been hiding long enough, sulking and stewing as the rest of the world went on without him. At some point, he had to get himself together. He had to face Society and the friends he had been avoiding and the future that now seemed wide open and utterly different than it had been in the years he was resigned to a loveless arranged marriage.

"What do you have in mind?" he asked, slow and uncertain.

Ewan and Matthew exchanged a grin before Ewan scribbled, *"There's a play tonight that you must see. Everyone is talking about it. Come out with us."*

Graham let out a long sigh. "I don't know. The theatre? That's a big leap from hiding out in pubs."

"We'll sneak in late," Tyndale assured him. "No one will have to know you're there unless you want them to. Come on. It's better than passing out behind some tavern and making Ewan and me carry you home, isn't it?"

Graham shot Ewan a look. He was a massive man, well over six feet and built out of pure muscle. "You've never carried anything home in your life, Tyndale, not if your cousin is with you."

As Ewan grinned, Matthew elbowed him and shot Graham a look. "Does that mean you'll go, bad company as you are?"

Graham nodded. "Yes. I'll do it." He sighed. "At least it will distract me."

The other two men looked happy at his decision as they all rose to leave the tavern, but Graham didn't feel the same. The last thing he wanted was to drag himself off to a public event where everyone could judge him. Not to mention waste a few hours watching some play that would probably be terrible.

But after all they'd done to support him, he owed it to his friends to try. And it was, after all, only one night.

Graham sat in a box overlooking the dark stage. Though he, Ewan and Tyndale had come into the theatre just before the rise of the curtain, it had not diminished the interest in his being there. Even now he felt the eyes of the crowd below on him, he'd heard the whispers of his name when he took his seat.

His cheeks and chest burned with humiliation and renewed anger. Thanks to Simon, his *friend*, the world pitied and judged and talked about him. He'd spent a lifetime trying to avoid anything that would make others do those very things and here he was.

Exactly where he didn't want to be, and he glanced at the exit behind him.

"Don't run," Ewan wrote, nudging him with an elbow to force him to read it in the dim light.

Graham folded his arms. Apparently he was becoming predictable. "I'm not going anywhere," he grunted as the lights on the stage rose and the curtain along with it.

He settled back to watch what would surely be a terrible performance, as many of these plays were. The theatre was more a place for those who wished to be seen, rather than for anything worth watching. But to his surprise, the usual din of noise of people chatting faded and everyone seemed to truly pay attention as a woman entered the stage.

He leaned forward as she began to speak. She was beautiful, with honey blonde hair that fell around her shoulders in waves. She had a fine, clear voice that carried even to the rafters. But what stood out most was her confidence. As she strode across the stage, it was impossible not to watch her every move.

"I pray for death," she said, her voice trembling with what felt like true emotion. "To free me from this pain. Strike me down, won't you? End this farce of a life."

Graham stared. She was *good*.

He watched for a while, enthralled as another actor came on stage and the woman turned toward him, her face twisted with emotion. The man was overshadowed by the light of her star. Eventually, he leaned in to Ewan and whispered, "Who is she?"

Ewan sent him a side glance and then wrote on his pad for a moment. When he turned it over to Graham, it read, *"Lydia Ford. She's the toast of London theatre at present. The reason why everyone wants to see this play."*

"Lydia," he repeated as he turned the notebook back to his friend. He stared at the lady again. She had turned her face and was looking up at the box, at him, though that was just a trick of the light. He knew she couldn't truly see him in the shadows.

"Beautiful," he whispered.

Next to him, he was aware that Ewan and Tyndale exchanged a look, but he didn't care. For the first time in what felt like forever, a heated interest had lit in his chest. A need for a woman. *This* woman. Lydia Ford.

And he wanted to meet her, to see if that desire would last longer than the duration of a play.

Lydia Ford sat on the settee in the dressing room behind the stage, mending a hole in one of her costumes and laughing with her understudy, Melinda Cross.

"I swear, Robin has to stop stabbing me so hard in that death scene," Lydia said as she shook her head. "Even a wooden sword hurts like a bugger and he keeps tearing the gown. Does he do the same to you on the nights when you play the role?"

"He's a clod but no, he's never put a hole in my gown." Melinda rolled her eyes. "I think he's just jealous that everyone comes to see *you* perform, not him."

Pride swelled in Lydia's chest at her friend's compliments, for she was gratified by her nights in the theatre. More to the point, she recognized how lucky she was to be able to do the work, given where she'd come from. Her two worlds couldn't be more different.

There was a light knock on the door and they both turned to see their stage manager, Toby Westin, open it. He was a tall, thin man with a nervous disposition and a sheet of paper covered with a never-ending list of things to do. "Lydia, you have someone who wishes to meet you."

Lydia shook out the gown she'd been repairing before she got to her feet. "Oh?" she asked as she hung the garment. She tried to sound nonchalant but dread rose in her chest.

One thing she had learned in her few short months as a star of the stage was that men flocked to actresses. Oh, none of them would dare go out in public with one, since any lady who walked the boards was considered hardly better than a whore, but in private they were drawn like moths to a flame.

Even during her short time as an actress she'd had several impertinent offers from merchant and gentleman alike and had turned them all down as kindly as she could manage when her stomach was turning.

"Please tell us it's not that awful Sir Archibald," Melinda interjected with a shudder. "He refuses to leave me alone no matter how often I turn down his disgusting advances."

Lydia gave her friend a supportive glance. No one liked the nasty Sir Archibald. He was a fixture at the theatre and pushed himself where he didn't belong whenever possible. He also grabbed the actress's behinds and made himself a general nuisance whenever he came backstage after a show.

"No," Toby said with a concerned glance for Melinda. "It's most certainly *not* Sir Archibald. *You* have caught the attention of a duke, Lydia."

She swallowed as the room began to spin and her ears started to ring. Using every bit of talent she had, she fought to keep her reaction from her face and gave Toby the smile she knew was expected of her.

"A duke, *really*? How...interesting."

"Interesting?" Melinda crowed. "You mean lucrative."

"Depending on the duke," Lydia corrected her softly. "Who is this man?"

"Northfield," Toby said, raising both eyebrows.

Melinda spun on her, her pretty face lit up with nothing short of glee. "The Duke of Northfield, Lydia, my goodness! You know who he is, don't you?" She didn't wait for the answer before she continued, "He's devilishly handsome for one, and young. *And* rich. He was engaged to some chit and his best friend stole the woman right out from under him. Since then he's been locked away."

Lydia swallowed hard. She knew *all* those things. Though from very different sources than Melinda had heard them. "Where do you get these rumors?" she asked, forcing a laugh past her dry throat.

Melinda grinned. "I, unlike you, care about Society, Lydia. A woman in my position ought to. There are many paths one can take to financial security."

Toby snorted and Lydia paced away as the two began the same argument they had at least once a week about actresses who became mistresses. Despite her aversion to Sir Archibald, Melinda wasn't opposed to becoming an important man's lover. She was always encouraging Lydia to consider the same option.

But Melinda only did that because she didn't know the truth. The truth that Lydia protected jealously and went to great lengths to hide. But now that the Duke of Northfield desired to meet Lydia all her work seemed poised on the edge of a precipice. He could destroy not only this world, but the other one she inhabited on a regular basis because if he was in a room with her he might *see* her. It was one thing to see her on stage, from far away, with bright lights making her seem like something she wasn't.

But closer up, Northfield might see the secret she struggled to keep every time she left the stage.

That secret was that she was *not* Lydia Ford. She was Lady Adelaide, the wallflower daughter of the long-dead Earl of Longford. A woman no one noticed, not even enough to realize she snuck out three times a week to become the city's most celebrated actress.

"So are you going to meet him?" Toby pressed.

Adelaide stared down at the hands she'd clenched before herself. They shook. How could she get out of this? "I'm not certain it's wise. Why not let him meet Melinda?"

Toby shook his head immediately and his frown deepened. "He was clear about what he wanted and he doesn't seem the kind of man one refuses. He wants to meet *you*, Lydia, and that's all that will satisfy him. I'm not certain he wouldn't just barge in here if I told him no."

Adelaide sighed. Of course, Toby was probably right. She'd been in Society all her life, she'd known many a man of power and privilege. And she'd had plenty of time to observe Northfield, as well, for he was hard to ignore. In a room full of men who were average, he was...*not*. Perhaps it was his piercing blue eyes or the hard edge to his expression or that he rarely danced, even with the lady who had once been his fiancé.

Whatever it was, Toby was correct in his assessment that Northfield *wasn't* the kind who took no for an answer.

She looked at herself in the mirror. She had changed into a plain gown, but she had not yet removed her stage makeup, and her hair was down. She still looked like Lydia rather than plain, mousy Adelaide. Perhaps Northfield wouldn't recognize her.

It wasn't as if he ever talked to her in Society anyway. There, *she* was a gnat and *he* was a god.

"It's good thing I still look presentable," she said with a sigh. "Yes, of course, allow him to come in."

Toby left to fetch the man and Melinda jumped up. "Oh, Lydia! What a night. Just think, you could advance your fortunes with just a few well-placed words."

Adelaide pursed her lips. "I'm perfectly content with my fortunes as they are, Melinda," she said. "I'm not trying to advance myself."

Melinda stared at her like she'd spoken Latin or grown a second head. "Not advance yourself?"

Adelaide laughed at her friend's confusion. "Gracious, Melinda, did it never occur to you that perhaps I just like walking the boards? That I'm not trying to do anything but enjoy the time I have to do so?"

"Well, to each his own." Melinda shook her head. "But I still say if you don't try to at least flirt with the man, you're wasting your time and a golden opportunity."

Adelaide sighed. "How about this? The moment he realizes I'm nothing but a boring mouse, I'll send him to you."

"Oh, do!" Melinda said on a laugh as there was a second knock on the door. This time it was harder, more confident, and Adelaide's heart sank. It was *him*.

Melinda shot her a final look and then opened the door, revealing the Duke of Northfield. And as she stared at him, trying not to reveal too much, trying not to fall over from nervousness, Adelaide's heart all but stopped.

ALSO BY JESS MICHAELS

The 1797 Club

The Daring Duke

Her Favorite Duke

The Broken Duke

The Silent Duke

The Duke of Nothing

The Undercover Duke

The Duke of Hearts

The Duke Who Lied

The Duke of Desire

The Last Duke

The Duke's By-Blows

The Love of a Libertine

The Heart of a Hellion

The Matter of a Marquess

The Redemption of a Rogue

The Shelley Sisters

A Reluctant Bride

A Reckless Runaway

A Counterfeit Courtesan

To see a complete listing of Jess Michaels' titles, please visit:
http://www.authorjessmichaels.com/books

ABOUT THE AUTHOR

USA Today Bestselling author Jess Michaels likes geeky stuff, Vanilla Coke Zero, anything coconut, cheese and her dog, Elton. She is lucky enough to be married to her favorite person in the world and lives in the heart of Dallas, TX where she's trying to eat all the amazing food in the city.

When she's not obsessively checking her steps on Fitbit or trying out new flavors of Greek yogurt, she writes historical romances with smoking hot characters and emotional stories. She has written for numerous publishers and is now fully indie and loving every moment of it (well, almost every moment).

Jess loves to hear from fans! So please feel free to contact her at Jess@AuthorJessMichaels.com.

Jess Michaels offers a free book to members of her newsletter, so sign up on her website:
http://www.AuthorJessMichaels.com/

facebook.com/JessMichaelsBks
twitter.com/JessMichaelsBks
instagram.com/JessMichaelsBks
bookbub.com/authors/jess-michaels

Made in the USA
Columbia, SC
27 September 2023

23471542R00128